Valerie's hand moved from Jackie's breast to between her legs . . . "God, I want you." Fingers slipped inside of her and began a gentle stroking. . .

"I can't do this standing up," Jackie said breathlessly. She felt like a rag doll, limp and submissive.

"Sure you can," Valerie whispered. Her fingers moved with precision and determination as she held her up with her other arm. "Come for me."

Titles by Peggy J. Herring

Available from Bella Books

Once More With Feeling

A Moment's Indiscretion

Calm Before the Storm

The Comfort of Strangers

Beyond All Reason

White Lace and Promises

A Moment's Indiscretion

Peggy J. Herring

Bella
BOOKS

Bella Books, Inc.
P.O. Box 10543
Tallahassee, FL 32302

First published 1998 by Naiad Press

Printed in the United States of America on acid-free paper
First Edition, Second Printing - November 2004

Editor: Lila Empson
Cover designer: Sandy Knowles

ISBN 1-931513-59-7

For Frankie

Acknowledgments

I'd like to thank Marge Reed for sharing her expertise on the Dominion. Very few know it the way she does.

I'd also like to thank Stacia for taking the time to answer my Harley questions.

And a special thanks to Frankie J. Jones, the love of my life, for her insight, attention to detail, and enthusiastic support. No one does it better.

PART I
Jackie

Chapter One

Jackie set her briefcase down and fumbled with the keys. With the porch light not working, she couldn't really see anything. She stuffed the pile of mail under her arm and searched for the lock in the dark. Having to call this place home for another month irritated her all over again. She nudged the door with her shoulder and finally got it open, but not without sending the mail flying in all directions.

"Wonderful," she mumbled.

Once inside she took off her heels and draped her jacket over the back of the sofa. As she switched on a lamp near the recliner, Jackie remembered that the light on the ceiling fan didn't work either. Glancing up at the cathedral-like peak in the middle of the living room, she sighed heavily and then decided it would take a ladder attached to a fire truck to reach the bulb up there. So much needed fixing in this place that even the *thought* of having to do it was overwhelming.

It had been a mistake not to rent out her father's house after his death five years earlier, but at the time Jackie hadn't wanted to deal with it. There were too many memories of him here as he suffered through the final stages of lung cancer. It had been easier to just lock the place up and forgot about it until taxes were due. And now that the house had been vacant for so long, the whole thing was falling down around her ears. There never seemed to be time for anything, and all she really wanted to do was get it fixed up enough to unload on someone else. At some point in the future she hoped to build another house, but she couldn't imagine a break in her schedule long enough to take care of the details.

She noticed her answering machine blinking in the corner and listened to her messages. Jackie laughed when she heard her friend Carla's voice.

"Before I leave for my Sex Without Partners support group meeting," Carla announced, "I thought I'd call and see if you could pencil me in for dinner on Thursday. Sevenish would be good. Call me with a yes or no."

The other messages were either work related or clever telephone solicitors hoping she wouldn't notice who they were. Jackie scribbled down what she needed from each message and then returned Carla's call.

"Sevenish on Thursday is good," she said when Carla answered. "Maybe Chinese this time."

"What's for dinner tonight?"

Jackie spied her briefcase on the sofa. "Work. The usual."

"Could you spare me thirty minutes?" Carla asked. "I'll pick up a pizza. Next week's my birthday and you promised

4

to throw me a big bash, remember? I'm sure you've got it planned already."

"Jesus, that's right." She glanced around her sparsely furnished living room with a renewed sense of distaste. Maybe she could get a few more things out of storage.

"A medium with everything, right?" Carla said. "I'll pick up some beer on the way."

Jackie scanned the room full of women and realized that she probably knew fewer than three people in attendance. Beer cans and empty cups were everywhere, and the majority of the food had disappeared hours ago. Most of the women were younger, but they seemed to be well acquainted with Carla. *Where the hell does she find them*, Jackie wondered. By two o'clock in the morning, she reached her limit. She kissed Carla on the cheek, wished her a happy birthday, and left her in the kitchen with two women.

"I'm going to bed," Jackie said sleepily on her way down the hall. "Either let yourselves out when you're finished or crash somewhere. And keep the noise down, okay?"

"It's still early," Carla protested.

"Tell me all about it tomorrow. I'm outta here."

Jackie woke up to the sun poking through the broken slats in the blinds at what appeared to be much too early already. *I wonder if the party's over yet*, was her first conscious thought. She woke up. She hadn't drunk anything the night before, but she felt as though she had. She stumbled over more empty beer cans and paper plates piled everywhere once she was downstairs. The kitchen was one big disaster as well.

With the coffee started, she began roaming through the house and filling a trash bag. In the living room she noticed various articles of clothing making a trail to one of the downstairs bedrooms where the door was open about halfway. Jackie dragged the trash bag along behind her and peeked in, finding Carla asleep and wrapped in a naked embrace around some as-yet-unidentified woman. The linen from the bed was scrambled evidence of their passion; Jackie shook her head and closed the door. A full trash bag later, Carla wandered into the kitchen with a sheet draped around her and short, dishwater-blond hair sticking out in all directions.

"Do I smell coffee?" Carla croaked. "Christ, I've got a headache."

"Who's your friend?"

"D.J.," Carla said. She took the cup Jackie handed to her. "Or is it Amy?" She blew on the coffee and then slurped at it loudly. "Amy or D.J. I don't remember which one got pissed and left." Carla glanced around the kitchen with half-opened eyes. "You cleaned already."

They both looked up as Carla's bedmate appeared in the doorway, now fully dressed in yesterday's clothes—tight gray jeans, a black tank top, and black leather boots. Her short, dark hair was neatly combed, and her teenage-boy's body looked very comfortable in her clothes. She was tall and had two endearing dimples that softened her face. Jackie decided that early twenties would be a generous estimate of her age.

"Good morning," the kid said as she leaned against the doorjamb. "You got a wrench or something?" she asked Jackie. "There's a bad leak in the bathroom sink."

Jackie eyed her for a moment to see if she was serious. "This whole house leaks."

"Water's a valuable resource," the kid said. "It shouldn't be wasted that way. Leaky faucets are a pet peeve of mine. If you've got the tools, I'll see what I can do."

"In the back," Jackie said, tossing a thumb over her shoulder. "There's an old workshop out there. Could be anything in it."

Jackie and Carla watched her leave through the back door. Carla leaned over and whispered urgently, "Which one is she? D.J. or Amy?"

"You're asking *me*? She's your friend."

"Shit. What good are you?" Carla hurried to the kitchen sink, still clutching the sheet around her nude body, and peered on tiptoe through the window. "She came with some friends of mine. I'd never met her before last night, but she's great in bed whoever she is."

Jackie chuckled and shook her head. "How can you sleep with someone and not even know her name?"

"I do know her name. It's either D.J. or Amy. Shhh! Here she comes!" Carla scurried back to the table and sat down.

"She looks like a D.J.," Jackie whispered as she pushed a lock of auburn hair away from her face. "Amy's one of those fluffy names. This one's out looking for a *wrench*, for crissakes."

"Shhh!"

The door opened, and the young woman came in carrying a large toolbox. "I found everything I'll need," she said. "I turned the water off outside. It shouldn't take long to fix."

"You want some coffee?" Jackie asked. *This is free labor*, she thought. *Be nice to it.* "What's your name by the way?" From her peripheral vision, Jackie could see Carla's sigh of relief.

7

"D.J. Roberts." She held the toolbox easily at her side, causing a nice bulge on her upper arm. Jackie knew for a fact that the toolbox was heavy because she'd attempted to move it off the dryer once. *When the dryer was working,* she reminded herself.

"Your back door sticks," D.J. said, "and the glass is broken out of a window in the workshop."

Jackie looked at her and mentally added *sticky back door* and *broken window in workshop* to the long list of repairs to be made. "My toilets run constantly, every faucet, tub, and showerhead has a steady stream, and two-thirds of the lights in this place don't work," Jackie said. "And those are just the things I *know* about."

D.J. laughed and then nodded. "Let me see what I can do with the leaks first, then we'll talk, okay?"

Jackie and Carla watched her amble down the hallway in the direction of the downstairs bathroom. They fixed another pot of coffee and shared some cinnamon toast. Jackie pointed at the sheet still securely wrapped around Carla's nude body and asked, "Were you planning on getting dressed today?"

"Eventually. Where's the aspirin?"

An hour later the water was back on and Jackie was given a tour of her new leak-free fixtures. She was impressed beyond words and beamed her appreciation. They returned to the kitchen where D.J. pulled out a chair and sat down at the table across from Carla, who was now also dressed in yesterday's clothes.

"Great party last night," D.J. said. "One I'll never forget."

Jackie noticed that Carla blushed appropriately.

"There's a lot of work that needs to be done around here," D.J. continued, "and I enjoy doing this type of thing. It just so happens that I'm having roommate problems right now and need a place to stay for a while." She tapped clean, squared nails rhythmically on the table and leaned back in her chair. "I noticed that the little workshop out back has a bed and a tiny bathroom. There's also a refrigerator in it. I'd like to suggest a deal for you."

"I'm not sure any of that stuff works," Jackie said. "It's probably been ten years since anyone's lived out there."

"Then let me fix that up, too," D.J. said, now leaning forward in the chair. "You need repairs, and I need a place to stay. It's as simple as that. We can give it a week and see what you think."

"Do you have a job?" Jackie asked bluntly. "A regular source of income?"

"A friend has a landscaping business. When she has work, I have work."

Jackie didn't have to think about it too long. A week's worth of free labor sounded like a damn good deal to her.

Jackie pulled into the driveway late Wednesday evening and noticed that the porch light was on. *My little handyperson's been earning her keep*, she thought with a smile. She collected her mail and unlocked the door without having to jiggle the key. The first thing that popped in her head once she set her briefcase down was that the living room light perched on the ceiling fan thirty feet in the air was working. Jackie kicked off her shoes and flipped the switch, instantly bathing the room in light. She sat down on the sofa and marveled at the difference it made in the room. D.J. Roberts had come through above and beyond already, and her week wasn't even up yet.

In the kitchen Jackie found a list of repairs that had been done that day. Receipts from the hardware store for parts were propped up next to the coffeepot. She totaled the receipts and wrote out a check, knowing that D.J. would pick it up in the morning. They seldom saw each other, but notes and daily transactions were successfully carried out this way. Jackie's eyes had already been trained to go directly to the coffeepot for some sort of correspondence every time she entered the kitchen.

The doorbell rang, and Jackie chuckled at the nice sound it made. She couldn't remember it ever working before.

Assuming that it was Carla at the door, Jackie answered it without preamble, ready to sing D.J.'s praises. But instead of Carla, it was Phyllis, Jackie's psychotic ex-lover, standing on the porch. Seeing her again sent a rush of panic coursing through Jackie's body. A string of police reports and a restraining order against her apparently weren't much of a deterrent any longer.

"I need a place to stay tonight and some money," Phyllis said as she nudged her way through the door. Jackie stood there stupidly holding it open for her, but once she got her wits together, she went directly to the telephone to call the police.

"What the hell are you doing?" Phyllis snapped as she yanked the phone away from her and hung it up again.

"Get out."

"I need a place to stay," Phyllis said. She moved closer and slowly backed Jackie into a wall. "Are you gonna help me or not?"

"How did you find me?"

There was that sick little smile—the smile that always made Jackie's blood run cold. Instant fear gripped her whole being.

"I followed you from work, sweetheart." Phyllis placed her hand on the wall beside Jackie's head and leaned into her. Their faces were only inches apart, and Jackie could smell the whiskey on her breath. "Did you actually think I couldn't find you if I wanted to?"

Jackie felt nauseous as panic surfaced. She heard a noise in the kitchen and wondered if Phyllis had brought someone with her.

"Is there a problem here?" Jackie heard D.J. say from the hallway near the kitchen.

Jackie took a deep breath and tried to keep from shaking. "She's just leaving," she whispered.

"You finally fuckin' somebody new?" Phyllis queried with that wicked smile as she dropped her hand from the wall. "She doesn't look like your type, Jackie old girl."

"Get out," Jackie said.

Phyllis didn't move until D.J.'s menacing voice uttered, "The lady said get out."

Phyllis slowly backed away, never taking her wild, green eyes off of her, and to Jackie's relief and surprise, Phyllis left quietly. After a moment D.J. asked if Jackie was okay.

"Yeah." Now that Phyllis was gone, she started to tremble uncontrollably.

"You sure?"

"I'm fine," she said, a little more gruffly than she'd intended. "Thanks. Really. I'm okay." She fumbled with the lock and then leaned her head against the front door. *She followed you from work, you dumb shit!*

"Who was that?"

Jackie turned around and rubbed her arms to keep from shaking even more. "A one-night stand that wouldn't go home. It's a long, stupid story." She went to the sofa and collapsed, propping her feet on the coffee table. "Thanks for showing up when you did. She's crazy as hell."

"You're afraid of her. Why'd you let her in?"

"I thought it was Carla."

"You're too trusting," D.J. said gently. "You should be more careful."

"Thanks for the hindsight. Now please leave me alone so I can get hysterical in private."

She heard the back door close as D.J. left, and Jackie leaned her head against the sofa. Later in bed that night, she jumped at every creak and pop that the old house teased her with. It was a long time before she fell asleep.

The next day, for the first time in two months, Jackie arrived home early from work. It was strange seeing the house in the daylight—she usually left every morning in the dark and didn't get home until very late. She found D.J. staining the outside of the privacy fence near the driveway. She had a Walkman clipped to her belt and earphones in place. They nodded to each other.

Carla called a bit later to see if Jackie wanted to go out for dinner, but even though Jackie had got home early, she still brought tons of work from the office.

"I've got too much to do," Jackie said. "Pick something up and come on over. I can spare you thirty minutes, I guess."

Carla unpacked cartons of potato salad and coleslaw before going to the sink to look out the kitchen window.

"She left already," Jackie said.

"Who?"

Jackie chuckled. "Who, my butt. D.J. Who else?"

"Do you think she's too young for me?"

"Not at all. As long as it's something you both want."

Halfway through dinner Jackie asked how old D.J. was.

"Twenty-four," Carla said with a crinkled nose. "I checked her driver's license the other night."

"You've got fifteen years on her," Jackie said. "That sounds like a lot, huh?"

"You think so?"

Jackie laughed again. "I'm kidding."

"You and I are about the same age," Carla said. "You think she's too young for you?"

"They're all too young for me, no matter how old they are."

Jackie heard a car pull up in the driveway and watched Carla hurry to the kitchen window again. "Is she alone?" Jackie asked.

Carla turned around with wide eyes. "Has she been taking other women back there?"

Jackie looked at her with raised eyebrows. "I'm kidding again. Jesus, Carla. Lighten up!"

"This isn't funny, damn it!" Carla folded her napkin and stuffed it in the trash can in the corner. Dusting her hands off she said, "I'm sure you've got work to do. I'll just leave you alone and go visit for a while."

The next morning when Jackie left for work she noticed that Carla's car was still in the driveway. *That's some visit*, she thought with a chuckle.

Chapter Two

Carla didn't think she had another one in her, but D.J. was a very thorough, diligent lover. They'd been at it for hours already, but Carla was not one to discourage such advances.

"I love that morning-after sex smell, don't you?" D.J. said later. She stretched out beside Carla and nuzzled her neck.

"Nothing better."

Just as they were beginning to settle down again, D.J. asked how long Carla and Jackie had been friends.

"Since college," Carla said. "Forever."

"Were you lovers?"

Carla laughed and kissed her on the chin. "Only for about ten minutes during our freshman year. We got stuck in a hailstorm in her car one night. We buttoned up as soon as the weather cleared, and neither one of us has mentioned it again."

D.J. sat up and readjusted her pillow against the head-board of the tiny bed. "Really? You've never talked about it?"

"Not a peep. I think we both realized that we make better friends than lovers. That doesn't take a genius."

D.J. pulled the sheet up around her better. "There was a woman who showed up over here a few nights ago wanting a place to stay. Any idea who it was?"

Carla felt a chill scamper up and down her arms. "What'd she look like?"

"About my height with short, red hair. A body builder, maybe. She looked good."

"Oh, shit," Carla said, and sat up quickly. "Did she have a butterfly tattoo on her arm?" At D.J.'s nod, Carla began to get really excited. "Christ! That was Phyllis! What happened? Tell me what happened!"

"I heard them arguing when I came in. Jackie was trying to get her to leave."

Carla held her head in her hands and rocked back and forth. "I thought Phyllis had left town for good. Jackie has a restraining order against her, and there should still be a warrant out for her arrest!"

"Why? What'd she do?"

Carla told her about meeting Phyllis at a health club a few years ago and then introducing her to Jackie. "She's got the worst luck of anybody I've ever known. Jackie's only had two real relationships in forty-two years, and both of these women were the biggest shits in the world!" Carla pulled the sheet up over her breasts and began telling D.J. about Jackie's first lover.

"They'd been together about a year, and things seemed to be okay. I never really liked Karen that much, but Jackie was happy and that was good enough for me. Karen goes away on a business trip, and two days later Jackie gets a call from Karen's mother saying that Karen had died. The funeral was in Dallas, and Jackie was absolutely devastated. It was horrible. I went with her and I will never forget it." She clutched the sheet tighter and then let go of it again. "A week later Jackie's still pretty out of it when she finds this man at her door. Apparently Karen hadn't gone on this business trip alone. She went with another woman, and, as it turns out, there hadn't been any business trip at all. They'd just gone away together for the weekend. Anyway, the man at the door turns out to be the coworker's husband! He tells Jackie that his wife and Karen had been lovers for several months and that they'd rented a cabin in the hill country for the weekend. It started raining real bad while they were there, and they got caught in a low-water crossing on the way back home. They were washed away and drowned." Carla shuddered. "Jesus, it was awful."

She sank into D.J.'s arms as the memory of how hurt Jackie had been still pierced her heart. "That was really rough," Carla whispered. "When she wasn't feeling betrayed and used, she was mourning the loss of her lover. It was bad, real bad, and Jackie's never got over it. Then," Carla said, her voice rising, "then I introduced her to Phyllis. Crazy, psycho Phyllis."

Carla ran a hand through her short blondish hair and then pulled her knees up to her chest before continuing. "Phyllis liked Jackie's money more than anything else. They were together almost three weeks before the real Phyllis showed herself. She was into drugs and started selling Jackie's things a piece at a time for more money. Phyllis couldn't hold a job, and she even hit Jackie once. That's what it took to really open Jackie's eyes." Carla reached over and took D.J.'s hand. "Before Jackie could throw her out, Phyllis emptied Jackie's house of absolutely everything. Loaded up a moving van and cleaned it out as soon as Jackie went to work one morning. She trashed the place, too. There was spray paint on the walls and carpet. It was terrible. Then," Carla said as she grabbed D.J.'s thigh at another memory, "it gets better. Then Phyllis calls up Jackie's boss and tells him she's a lesbian! Can you believe that?"

"Sweet Jesus," D.J. whispered.

"Jackie was in real bad shape after that. Real bad shape."

"Did she lose her job?"

"No," Carla said, "but things sure as hell weren't easy. She's just now gaining some of that ground back."

"She seems to be such a nice person."

"She can be," Carla agreed. "And she can be tough, too. The minute Jackie thinks you're taking advantage of her, she'll be all over your ass, honey."

D.J. hugged her.

"She's been shit on by the best," Carla said, "and she won't ever let it happen again. Jackie Knovac is a woman scorned." She kissed D.J.'s cheek and then pulled her down on top of her. "I'm out of the matchmaking business these days. Believe me. Crazy Phyllis cured me of that." She kissed D.J. tenderly on the mouth. "Now come here and show me how much you've missed me."

❧

Jackie found D.J.'s note propped up against the coffeepot first thing Saturday morning. Apparently they needed to discuss painting the inside and outside of the house, and what, if any, landscaping she wanted done. They'd come to an agreement to extend this free rent for free labor arrangement until the renovations on the house were complete. Jackie peered out the window over the kitchen sink and saw D.J. with a screwdriver, fixing the gate to the backyard.

"Good morning," Jackie said from the porch, shading her eyes from the sun. "Paint," she called and waved the note. "You paint, too, I take it."

D.J. grinned. "I do it all, ma'am."

"Okay," Jackie said. "Let's keep it easy then. White inside and the usual white with green trim on the outside."

"Easy enough." D.J. stuck the screwdriver in her back pocket and tried the latch on the gate again. "What about landscaping? Your grass is all dead from neglect, and you don't have any live trees left."

"Nothing with leaves," Jackie said. "I'm not a leaf raker, so I assume other people aren't either. And I never remember to water. That's what happened to the grass." She looked around the yard and tried to appear interested in it. "I guess I need something pretty self-sufficient. Like cactus. Shady cactus maybe. I don't know. You put it in and don't make me decide anything, and I'll like it even better."

"How much do you want to spend on the yard?" D.J. asked.

"What can I get for five hundred?"

"A real nice start."

Jackie laughed. "That's your budget. Five hundred." On her way back inside, she called over her shoulder, "And use my money wisely, young lady."

19

Jackie's heels clicked down the hallway back to her office where she expected new graphics and a pile of stats to be waiting for her on her desk. No more than a glance told her that they weren't there yet. She snatched up the phone and called her assistant.

"Tell me I'm overlooking them, Buzz."

"Sorry. They're saying another hour."

"We don't have another hour!"

"I can give you some dummy numbers to bullshit the big guy with this afternoon," Buzz said, "but real numbers won't be available for at least an hour. We need another person, Jackie. I'm all tied up with this little stuff, and I can't get to the real work."

Jackie reached for her empty coffee cup. "I don't bullshit well, Buzz, and you know that."

"You bullshit great," he said sincerely. "It's just that you don't like doing it."

She sighed but made a quick decision. "Then give me something good. We'll go over everything at lunch. The usual place at the usual time." She hung up and took her cup to the break room for her second cup of coffee. She both hated and loved deadlines. *If having to be creative under pressure is what's keeping me young, then I should be a damn embryo by now*, she thought wearily.

Jackie sprinkled in a little artificial sweetener and stirred the right amount of creamer into her cup. She didn't have time for any of this, but her part of the project couldn't be accomplished until everyone else came through. She passed by the three boxes of doughnuts and scanned their contents for the kind with the handle. She didn't find what she was looking for, so she went back to her office to make more phone calls.

Lunch was the usual huge table at the cafeteria on the third floor of their building. At least one briefcase per person was the norm.

"Do we have graphics yet?" Jackie asked as she glanced at her checklist next to the lukewarm bowl of soup.

"Graphics," Buzz said. He pulled out a folder and passed it over to her. His crew cut had grown out on top where he'd begun spiking it. He was one of the few men in the office who looked comfortable in a suit and tie. "We're strong on graphics. It's harder to bullshit a visual aid, so I had them concentrate a little more in that area."

Jackie sighed, her shoulders slumping ever so slightly at the reminder that she wouldn't be adequately prepared for the presentation. "I really hate this," she said.

"We need another person," Buzz reiterated. "They've given us more to do and less to do it with."

Jackie looked over at him as he took a bite of a bean sprout and avocado sandwich. He was young, late twenties, single, and would probably be in line for Jackie's position when she finally got her next promotion. She liked Buzz Metzger; they worked well together. He had covered her butt more than once when she'd needed him to, and hopefully he'd be able to do it again today.

"Just ask for somebody," he said. "They might surprise you."

"I'll see what I can do." She glanced at her checklist again. Getting authorization to hire another person shouldn't be a problem, but who the hell had time to do it?

The moment she walked into the house that evening, Jackie could smell the lingering odor of fresh paint. It wasn't bad enough to have to leave, but it wasn't a pleasant smell either. She took her heels off and went to the coffeemaker to see what words of wisdom D.J. had left for her today. Apparently one bedroom and the downstairs bathroom had been painted already.

Turning her computer on, she then listened to her telephone messages. She took a stack of papers out of her briefcase and set them on the coffee table. She looked up as D.J. came out of the downstairs bedroom with paint smudges on her strikingly handsome face.

"I put the furniture all back," D.J. said. "You're home early."

"I decided to bring it all with me instead of staying at the office."

"Carla's coming over later. Would you like to eat with us?"

Jackie smiled knowingly and declined the offer. Carla had been over every night this week. "I'll just nuke something later. Thanks."

"You're in advertising," D.J. said. She pulled a rag from her back pocket and tried rubbing at the dried paint on her fingers. "I've got a friend looking for a job in that field."

"Really?" Jackie took off her blazer and draped it over the back of a chair. "It just so happens that I got another position authorized today. If your friend's interested, then have him or her get in touch with personnel tomorrow. They'll need a current resume."

D.J. smiled. "I'll do that. Thanks." At the door to the kitchen she stopped and said, "Sure you won't join us for dinner later?"

"No, thanks. By the way, I haven't found any receipts by the coffeepot lately. Are you donating the paint?"

"Receipts are out back. You'll have them in the morning."

Three days later Buzz took Valerie Dennison around the office and introduced her to everyone. She was to be his assistant, which put her directly on Jackie's team. Buzz had interviewed her and was utterly enthralled by their good fortune.

"She's got a master's from Trinity," he said jubilantly. "We tripped and absolutely fell into this one."

Valerie Dennison was twenty-four, tall—about Jackie's height—with dark brown curly hair reaching past her shoulders. She was attractive and had an engaging smile. Within the first three hours of her arrival, the majority of the male population on the fifth floor had already attempted to find out everything there was to know about her. They passed tidbits of information back and forth in between trips to the water cooler and the break room. Any new female on staff was usually ogled in the most discreet ways possible, and Jackie took great pleasure in catching them at it when she could. The men stayed within bounds of any reasonable sexual harassment criteria, but only because Jackie constantly reminded them about how serious the consequences would be. Valerie Dennison, on the other hand, seemed oblivious to the attention and didn't appear to be encouraging anyone.

For a fleeting moment that first day, right after meeting Valerie Dennison, Jackie's sympathy went out to whoever D.J.'s friend was—the one looking for a job. There had been ten applicants for the new position, nine of whom were still out there hitting the pavement somewhere with a fresh resume in hand. *Starting a new job really sucks*, Jackie remembered with a cringe.

"She's good," Buzz said a few days later. "We'll have time to smooth out the details now."

Jackie didn't see much of Buzz or Valerie during the next week, but she noticed completed work finally beginning to appear on her desk at a steady rate. Sheets of statistics arrived with a Post-it note attached from Buzz stating, "Real thing. No bullshit." *This is much better*, Jackie thought. *I need to take them both to lunch soon. My treat.*

She instructed Buzz that briefcases wouldn't be necessary, that they'd be eating, not working, at lunch today. Buzz informed her later that a few other people had asked to go along with them, and Jackie was amazed when she went downstairs at noon. Six men from accounting had joined them.

Jackie took a seat across from Valerie and realized that this wasn't at all what she had intended, but as time went on Jackie found her irritation gradually waning. She noticed Valerie's quick wit and her ability to use it appropriately on several occasions. And a few times during the meal Valerie said something amusing enough to set the whole table off in

24

a roar of laughter. It was obvious that at least four of the men were truly infatuated with her, and only two of them, Jackie noted, were single.

"Buzz tells me you're a runner, Ms. Knovac," Valerie said.

Jackie was startled at hearing her last name used before she remembered that they hadn't said more than two words to each other since Valerie had started working there.

"Please call me Jackie," she said, meeting those piercing brown eyes. "I don't have time to run anymore," Jackie explained as she took a sip from her water glass and smiled. "I guess I should say I don't take the time."

"I've been running before work the last few days," Valerie said. "They have nice shower facilities on fourteen if you'd like to give it a try in the morning. I'm usually here by six."

Jackie noticed how a few ears across the table perked up. She smiled again. Tomorrow there'd be joggers everywhere hoping to catch a glimpse of Valerie Dennison in skimpy shorts.

"I'm not really a morning person," Jackie said. The thought of getting up early and dragging her clothes and miscellaneous running paraphernalia to work didn't appeal to her at all, no matter how skimpy Valerie Dennison's shorts promised to be.

All through lunch their eyes kept meeting, and Jackie sensed a flicker of attraction between them. She nudged that thought out of the way and abruptly snatched up the bill and paid it.

◈

Over the next few days Jackie received several compliments from the boss on her team's work. "Having an extra person has helped," she said.

"We need to massage this Flanagan account for a while," Mr. Jamison said. "The downtown office almost lost it for us. Rebuilding Flanagan's confidence will take some work, but it looks like you've got a good team. I like what I see here, Jackie." He thumped the folder on his desk and nodded.

His deep rumbling voice and naturally gruff nature unsettled most people, but Jackie knew him to be a very fair and knowledgeable department head. He'd been sympathetic when Phyllis had called him up in the middle of the night almost four years ago to announce Jackie's preference for women, and at the time Jackie had been prepared to clean out her desk and pack up her office. In addition, Phyllis had taken it upon herself to also phone several coworkers that dreadful night, so word of Jackie's lesbianism had been all over the office the following morning.

Jackie and the boss spoke of Phyllis only once after that, and Mr. Jamison informed her then that he didn't care what Jackie did on her own time. Any damage done to her future with the company was more or less only in Jackie's mind, but it had still been a very humiliating experience. She'd never been embarrassed about or ashamed of being a lesbian, but deciding who should know and when to tell them was a personal choice that should've been Jackie's decision to make.

"Keep up the good work," Mr. Jamison said as he rose from his desk. Jackie nodded and left his office.

⁂

A few days later she had plans to take Buzz and Valerie to lunch again to pass on the boss's praise. She also wanted to express how much she appreciated their hard work. On her way to Buzz's office, Jackie heard deep male laughter in the hallway and knew instinctively that Valerie was the cause of it. Like a pack of wolves getting a whiff of a seasoned female, they seemed to search Valerie out no matter where she was. Jackie's position in the company was high enough that her unexpected presence at a gab session in the hallway would immediately dissolve such a cluster, and this time was no exception.

After the drooling accountants had gone, Jackie said to Valerie, "If you and Buzz are free, I'd like to take both of you to lunch again." She smiled. "An eating lunch, not a working lunch."

Valerie nodded. "Fine. The usual time?"

"Yes." Back in her office Jackie wondered how much of her personal life was still part of the office grapevine. *You're paranoid, Knovac,* she thought tiredly. *Maybe you're old news in these parts now.*

Jackie really didn't know exactly when it all started, but one afternoon in particular set itself apart in her mind. On this particular day Mr. Jamison was springing for lunch for everyone in the department, and Jackie noticed how Valerie made it a point to sit next to her. The long table was crowded with close to thirty people, and whenever Valerie had something to say to her she would lean over and lightly touch Jackie's arm. Jackie was very aware of their closeness, and if this was flirting, then it seemed innocent enough to be nonthreatening, but after Jackie's initial surprise at how much she liked it, her defense shields snapped into place quickly.

During the remainder of the luncheon, Jackie kept the conversation safely generic and totally work related. There had been a few other times recently, especially during briefings in the conference room, that Jackie noticed how Valerie made it a point to at least sit across from her if seats beside Jackie were already taken. Other women always attended these briefings, women that Valerie worked with during the day and obviously got along with quite well. *She's a part of your team, Knovac,* Jackie reminded herself. *It's only natural that she go out of her way to sit with you.*

The reports on Valerie's work from other sections were all excellent. Jackie knew how lucky she was to have someone who had been able to come into the office with little more than a few days of training and be fully functional. That in itself was virtually unheard of.

One afternoon several days later Buzz and Jackie were working on a deadline when Buzz had to be pulled for another project.

"Valerie can do it," he said as he tossed folders into his briefcase. He'd been preaching about her capabilities for five minutes already.

Afterward Jackie went to Valerie's office to explain exactly what she needed and when she needed it. She stood beside her desk, nearly losing her concentration as Valerie's perfume heightened her awareness of how close they were. Jackie was brief and waited a moment for questions that never came. The project was on her desk an hour early, looking better than anything else Jackie could have hoped for.

"The Flanagan account," Jackie said a few days later when she poked her head in Valerie's office. "Will we or won't we have anything today?"

"Doesn't look like it," Valerie said. "The system's down."

Jackie rested her head against the door and groaned. Valerie reached over to answer her telephone and listened for a moment before saying, "Okay. Thanks," and then hung up. "We won't be back online until after six."

Jackie groaned again.

"I can stay and get what we need," Valerie offered. She tossed her light brown curly hair off her shoulder with a flick of her wrist. She truly didn't seem to notice the effect she had on people. "Are you working at home later?"

"Unfortunately," Jackie said.

Valerie looked up at her. "I can bring you whatever I get. We should at least have enough to make you sound competent by tomorrow morning."

"I don't bullshit well," Jackie reminded her. She smiled at Valerie's laughter. "Let me give you my address. I really appreciate this."

At home Jackie was grateful that D.J. hadn't started painting the living room yet. She didn't have time to deal with the clutter and the smell. Carla arrived with enough pizza for three, but Jackie declined, having no wish to see them making goo-goo eyes at each other or, even worse, having to endure another meal where they fed each other morsels from a shared paper plate. Jackie promised to pop "a something" in the microwave later if she got hungry, but she insisted that they make themselves at home while their pizza was still warm.

Valerie arrived at eight-thirty with the reports Jackie needed, and to Jackie's utter amazement, D.J. and Valerie hugged and chattered on for several minutes. Valerie said her good-byes a while later, and Jackie called D.J. back in the living room.

"You two know each other?"

"Valerie's the friend I told you about, remember? The one looking for a job."

"Oh, goodness," Jackie said, wondering why it hadn't occurred to her that D.J. and Valerie would know each other. "Well, you were absolutely right. She's good." Jackie didn't have the nerve to ask if Valerie was a lesbian, even though it was becoming much more obvious to her that she was. "How well do you know her?"

D.J. laughed. "We were in business together for a while. Ever heard of Flash Cubes? The ice-delivery service?"

Jackie nodded, remembering seeing the small blue trucks darting in and out of traffic all over town.

"Valerie owns it. I managed it for her last summer."

"Hmm."

"She's got a good head for business," D.J. said. "She also told me you're a great boss, by the way."

"She's a lesbian," Jackie finally said, letting the idea sink in very slowly. *Those are passes she's been tossing your way, dumb shit.*

D.J. smiled. "Oh, absolutely."

"Hmm."

The following evening Jackie came home from work early and found DYKE spray-painted in huge black letters across the front of her house. Sitting in her driveway with the motor running and her eyes filling with tears, she was paralyzed with anger, but she eventually got out of the car in a daze and opened the garage door. She found the white paint D.J. had been using for the inside of the house and grabbed a brush from a workbench.

There was no doubt in her mind that this was more of Phyllis's doing. Jackie's neighbors were coming home from work also, and cars in the street slowed as they passed the house. She was oblivious to everything and carelessly dripped paint on her brown suede heels and down the front of her skirt. She wiped the tears away on the sleeve of her yellow blouse and stoically piled the paint on as thick as she could. Minutes later she vaguely heard car doors slamming in the driveway.

"Who the hell would do something like this?" D.J. screeched.

"Phyllis," Carla said, her hand on Jackie's shoulder. "Give me the brush, baby," she said softly. Carla was crying too.

"Take her inside," D.J. said. "I'll finish this."

Jackie didn't remember much about going in the house. All she really knew was that she wanted to be alone. She sent Carla away and then took a shower. She scrubbed the paint from her hands and arms, and then got dressed in soft, faded jeans and a sweatshirt before throwing her paint-stained skirt and shoes away.

She had no idea how long she sat there in the dark, occasionally crying and sipping the Scotch she'd poured. Phyllis was obviously a mistake Jackie wasn't quite through paying for yet. Another call had probably already been placed to the boss again, stirring that up once more. Just the thought made the tears flow steadily.

A while later Carla came in through the back door using D.J.'s key. She switched on a lamp near the sofa, flooding the room with unwanted light. She nodded toward the glass of Scotch Jackie held.

"I thought you gave that up."

Jackie squinted over at her but didn't say anything.

"We found her," Carla said. She collapsed on the sofa and ran her hand through her short blond hair. "She's leaving town again."

"She wasn't by chance driving a moving van when you saw her, was she?"

Carla laughed softly and shook her head. "I don't think you'll be bothered by her again. D.J. put the fear of the Goddess in her. And by the way," she said with a devious smile, "Phyllis says the only reason you kept her around as long as you did was because the sex was so good."

Jackie glanced over at her with a hard, piercing look. "Once a week doesn't constitute good sex, no matter how good it is."

Carla chuckled and stuck her hand in her pocket and peeled off a fifty-dollar bill. She dropped it on the table. "D.J. made her pay for the paint and the labor."

Jackie eyed the bill for a moment. "Give it to D.J. I don't want Phyllis's money."

Carla got up and patted Jackie's shoulder. "I'll tell her it's here." She hugged her and then gave her a kiss on top of the head before turning the light out again.

"And don't smack my trash can on the way to your car at three in the morning," Jackie grumbled over her shoulder. "Get a flashlight, for crissakes."

32

Chapter Three

Jackie was impressed at how well she functioned on so little sleep, and made it a point to seek the boss out first thing to see if any new bulletins on her sexuality had been broadcast. She hated surprises. Her brief encounter with Mr. Jamison in the elevator, however, eased her fears. He was his usual grumpy morning self.

"I'll have a summary of the Flanagan presentation for you by nine-thirty," Buzz said as he passed her in the hallway. Jackie grunted an answer.

She opened her briefcase once she was in her office and noticed her coffee cup, already filled with coffee, in the middle of her desk with a Dunkin' Donuts doughnut sitting precociously beside it on a fresh white napkin. Jackie moved a little closer and touched the cup to check the temperature of the coffee. It was hot and looked as though the right amount of creamer had been added.

She went to her door and stuck her head outside, but didn't see anyone. Her secretary wasn't in yet, but she had never been one to attend to Jackie's coffee needs. Everyone fended for themselves in that area—even the boss could be found with his empty cup in the break room at any given hour of the day. Curiosity getting the best of her, Jackie returned to her desk and picked up the cup. *Phyllis could've sneaked in here and left this for you, idiot! She'd get a real kick out of poisoning you.*

Jackie headed for the ladies' room to dump the coffee out, and it also occurred to her to throw the cup away while she was at it. All sorts of wild things were going through her head as she met Valerie in the hall.

"Is it the way you like it?" Valerie asked. "It was fresh. I thought you might like some first thing."

Jackie nodded toward the cup. "You left this?"

"And the doughnut. The kind with the handle, right?" Valerie said. She waved at someone coming out of the elevator, then turned her attention back to Jackie. "The doughnuts were still warm when I picked them up this morning."

Jackie was in shock, but she recovered nicely after a moment. "I'm perfectly capable of getting my own coffee. I'm sure you have plenty to do without waiting on me." She smiled, hoping to soften the sting a bit. "And if you don't have enough to do, then I can take care of that, too."

"I'm almost finished with the stats for the Flanagan presentation," Valerie said, looking her squarely in the eye. Apparently no offense had been taken. "I'll have them to

Buzz shortly. And I'm sure you're quite capable of a lot of things, Ms. Knovac."

Someone called Valerie's name, and with that she was gone. Jackie stood there alone, holding her cup full of coffee. She blew on it and took a cautious sip.

"I'll be damned," she mumbled. The right amount of sweetener had been added also. It couldn't have tasted better if she had made it herself.

Buzz popped in a while later and got comfortable in one of the two chairs in Jackie's office. "The boss wants Valerie to help out in the downtown office," he said in frustration. "He needs her for about three days."

"What's going on downtown?"

"Another big account is ready to fall on its face and they're shorthanded. He heard how good she is and wants her."

Jackie shrugged. "Can we live without her for a few days?"

"Not without working our collective butts off!" Buzz pulled at the ends of his blond mustache. "She's great, Jackie. She's even offered to help after hours. On her own. There's no money in the budget for overtime this quarter."

"That won't be necessary, will it?" Jackie worked late without compensation, and Buzz could also be seen at the office during all hours. Such dedication from junior employees, however, was neither expected nor encouraged.

He shrugged. "I don't think so."

"If he likes her and she does well over there, they might decide to keep her," Jackie said quietly.

Buzz frowned. "Yeah, I thought about that."

"Does she realize what this could mean to her future here with the company?"

"I'm sure she does." He stood up and straightened his tie. "I guess we've been lucky to have her this long."

By mid-morning the next day, Jackie noticed how much she missed seeing Valerie out and about in the office. Apparently they were together more than she realized. At meetings there was an empty chair beside her, and trips down the hallway during the day were definitely missing something. *How often do I usually see her?* she wondered. *And how can I miss seeing someone I never even knew I was looking for?*

A few days later the boss requested everyone's presence at another luncheon. Jackie arrived a little late, but was pleasantly surprised to see Valerie there. The only seat left at the huge table was beside her.

"How's life downtown?" Jackie asked.

"Quiet."

"It's good that Mr. Jamison recognizes your potential."

Valerie glanced at her and asked very simply, "When will you recognize my potential?"

A bit flustered, Jackie unfolded her napkin and placed it in her lap. "I already do. Buzz has nothing but praise for your work."

"I wasn't talking about my work."

Jackie wasn't quite sure what to say after that, but before she had time to significantly recover, Valerie was lassoed into a conversation with the head of accounting sitting across the table from them.

A few minutes later Valerie leaned over and whispered, "I have some ideas I'd like to run by you. Could we discuss them over dinner tonight?"

Jackie dropped her fork on her plate, making a terrible clanking racket. She picked it up and realized that she momentarily had everyone's attention. "Uh," she started, and then laughed nervously. "Why don't you just run them by me now?"

Before either of them got any further with this, Mr. Jamison called out Valerie's name from the other end of the table and went on to acknowledge her for doing such a good job at the downtown office. The longer Jackie sat there, the more uncomfortable she became. It was obvious that someone had been talking to Valerie about her—either the regular office gossip or more likely D.J. Jackie left the luncheon as soon as she could without drawing any attention to herself. She returned to her office and informed her secretary that she was working on a project and didn't want to be disturbed.

At home that evening when Jackie got in, she found D.J. in the backyard planting a few shrubs. There was only about twenty minutes' worth of light left as Jackie sat on the porch and watched her work.

"How does buffalo grass around the pool sound?" D.J. asked. She had dirt smudges all over her face and sweat glistening off her arms and neck.

"Never heard of it," Jackie said.

"It's a hardier grass. Doesn't need as much water."

Jackie leaned back on her elbows. "Do they sell AstroTurf for yards?" she asked. "I wouldn't have to get it mowed then."

D.J. smiled and rolled her eyes, continuing to take care of the shrub. "Yeah, I know. As long as I don't make you decide anything, you'll like it even better, right?"

They heard a car door, and D.J. got up and dusted herself off a little. "That should be Carla. Tell her I'm getting cleaned up."

In the kitchen over diet sodas, Carla and Jackie sat around the table waiting for D.J. Jackie felt a million miles away. *Was Valerie actually asking me out to discuss work?* she wondered. Carrying on for the past three years as if that part of her life were over had been so easy. Now suddenly she felt unsettled and disoriented.

"I think I want to ask D.J. to move in with me," Carla said. "What do you think?"

"Have you talked to her about it?"

"Indirectly."

Jackie shrugged. "You already know what I think. You're setting yourself up for a fall."

"Thanks for the support."

Jackie laughed. "You asked for my opinion."

"And you give me a cynical pile of crap," Carla said. "So you made a few bad choices. Why should everybody else have to suffer for it?"

Jackie snatched up her glass and took a drink. "Fucking my gardener doesn't make you an expert on anything."

Carla pushed her chair back and glared at her across the table. "Not fucking at all doesn't make you one either."

Jackie got up and set her glass in the sink. "I'm sorry. I've had a shitty day, and I shouldn't be taking it out on you." She turned around and folded her arms across her chest. "And D.J. is more than just a gardener. She's been a good friend." Jackie sighed. "I haven't seen you this serious about anyone in a long time, Carla. Maybe I'm jealous that you've found somebody. We've both got lousy track records when it comes to relationships."

They looked up as D.J. came in the back door with semi-wet hair neatly combed in place.

Jackie smiled shyly. "That moose grass you were talking about earlier sounds fine."

D.J. laughed and reached for Carla's hand. "It's buffalo grass, not moose grass. I'll have some delivered tomorrow."

En route to the office the next morning, Jackie made a decision to explain her personal policy about work and socializing to Valerie. It seemed best for all concerned that they get this cleared up right away. They had to work together. A personal relationship with a coworker, much less a subordinate, would only complicate things.

Before Jackie could do much more than set her briefcase down, Mr. Jamison stuck his head in her office and told her that he needed everything on the Flanagan account by eleven.

Jackie paled. "Eleven today?"

"Eleven today. That's as close as I dare cut it. I'm briefing Flanagan myself at two o'clock downtown. Don't disappoint me."

Jackie had her secretary find Buzz and Valerie. She wanted them in the conference room with anything and everything they had on the Flanagan account.

A few minutes later Valerie pushed the conference room door open with her foot. In her arms she had a mountain of folders and charts. On her second trip in she brought a laptop computer and more files.

"Buzz is sick," she said. "He's at home, going at both ends."

Jackie paled again. "No. Please. This can't be happening."

"He's got several things on his computer. He knows we'll be calling him." Valerie looked over at her and smiled. "Relax. He's very organized. We'll do fine."

The two of them worked steadily together all morning. Graphics came through when they said they would, and statistics were available from another department as soon as Jackie asked for them. By ten they were leisurely proofing everything for the second time and could stop long enough to take a deep breath.

"We did it," Jackie said. Even now she had no idea why she loved deadlines so much. The adrenaline almost made her crazy at times.

"You had doubts," Valerie said. "I saw panic in your eyes at eight-thirty."

"*Panic* is a pretty strong word."

"Maybe we should celebrate," Valerie said. She put several folders in order and then studied Jackie carefully. "Since my dinner suggestion wasn't well received, maybe we could go to lunch someplace special. How about Saturday?"

Jackie began nervously shuffling papers. "Buzz might be back tomorrow. We can go then." *I need to put a stop to this*, she thought.

"You don't like being alone with me, do you?" Valerie said. Jackie stopped fiddling with the papers but was momentarily speechless.

"Why is that, Ms. Knovac?"

Jackie stood up and tucked the finished report under her arm. "I never socialize with coworkers," she said. Their eyes met again, and Jackie willed herself to hold the look longer than she felt comfortable with. "And that's the last time I'll explain myself to you."

"Is this job all that's keeping us from spending time together?"

Jackie didn't answer as she collected the charts and gathered up the graphics. "We're finished with this conversation." They both had their arms full as they moved toward the door.

"Is it the job?" Valerie asked again. Her voice was low and serious. "Please just answer my question." At the door she shifted the laptop to her other arm. "If we didn't work together—"

"What's the point of this, Valerie? We do work together. Now let's drop it."

"So it is the job."

Jackie was out the door and striding down the hall to the boss's office. *You certainly handled that well, idiot*, she thought wearily. She set the report on the boss's desk an hour early and returned to her office.

Twenty minutes later the hallway was a swarm of whispering, excited people. Everyone was there, and absolutely no work was getting done anywhere.

"What's going on?" Jackie asked her secretary.

"Valerie Dennison just quit. Walked right in the boss's office and resigned!"

"Quit? You're kidding. Where is she?"

"Gone already."

Two minutes later the boss wanted to see her. "Sit down," he said. Jackie eased into the chair in front of his desk. "A very strange thing just happened," he said with a frown.

"I heard that Valerie Dennison quit."

Mr. Jamison looked at her with a confused, lost expression on his face. "I asked her what the problem was, and she said"—he stopped and leaned back in his chair—"she said that she thought it would be better for all concerned if she was no longer employed here. Explain to me what exactly that means, Jackie. Did something happen with the Flanagan account? The two of you were working on it this morning."

Jackie cleared her very dry throat. "You'll have to ask her."

He sat up in his chair and ran his hand over his tired face. "I did, and she had nothing to say. Now I'm asking you."

Jackie could feel the heat slowly rising in her face. She took a deep breath to try and calm down.

"Did something happen this morning that I should know about?" he asked. "Six months down the road I don't want this coming back to bite us in the ass, Jackie."

"The project is ready an hour early," she said slowly, patiently. "What did Valerie say to you before she left?"

Mr. Jamison shrugged. "She said that you and Buzz were the best people she'd ever worked with, but she no longer felt that she could contribute anything to the company."

"Then let's take her at her word and get on with it. I'm sorry, but I can't help you."

When Jackie got home she had a mega headache and a message from Valerie on her answering machine.

"We're no longer coworkers," Valerie's smooth voice said from the small black machine. "Please reconsider that dinner invitation." Jackie went to the bathroom to get some aspirin. The phone rang before she got back.

"Hello," she said.

"This is Valerie. Did you get my message?"

Jackie sat down on the sofa and propped her feet up. "That was a crazy thing you did today."

"It doesn't feel crazy."

"Mr. Jamison called me in his office after you left. He probably thinks you resigned because I made a pass at you."

Valerie laughed. "Then I'll be in his office bright and early to tell him otherwise. I could even tell him the truth this time."

"Which is?" Jackie asked, surprised at how calm she felt and sounded. For some reason Valerie's voice was like a sedative.

"I could tell him that I had to quit because you wouldn't make a pass at me."

Jackie laughed for the first time all day. "Not a good idea."

"But it's true."

Jackie chose to ignore the connotations of this line of thinking. "If you need a recommendation for another job, I'll gladly give you one. I'm sure Buzz will too."

"Thanks. I might take you both up on that." After a moment, Valerie asked if she'd have dinner with her tomorrow night. "We don't work together any longer."

"I can't even begin to tell you how flattered I am by all of this," Jackie said honestly. It was the first time she allowed herself to admit it. "Jobs aren't that easy to get these days, and you had a good chance to go somewhere with the company."

"Maybe there was something else I wanted more," Valerie said.

Jackie allowed a little tingle to scamper through her body at that particular suggestion.

"I'll pick you up tomorrow at seven," Valerie said. "Dress casual and warm. I have a surprise for you."

After Jackie hung up, she was amused at how excited she felt. *It's just dinner, for crissakes,* she thought with a chuckle. *She'll be off playing with women her own age before I know it.*

The next day at the office, Buzz couldn't believe that Valerie was gone.

"You let her quit?" he roared. "I'm out sick one day and look what happens! What the hell are we supposed to do now?"

"How many people did you interview to begin with?" Jackie asked him patiently.

"Six or seven. Jesus, Jackie! This is all we need!"

"Were any of the other candidates suitable? Maybe they haven't found jobs yet." She came around her desk and gave him a friendly pat on the shoulder. "Call personnel and have them set up more interviews. We might get lucky again."

Chapter Four

Jackie heard an unfamiliar rumble and then a short while later the doorbell. She glanced at her watch and was pleased to see that it was seven sharp.

"Was that you making all that noise?" Jackie asked as she held the door open.

Valerie came in tousling her long curly hair. She was wearing brown denim pants and a tan corduroy button-down shirt. Jackie had never seen her in anything but skirts and dresses but could easily imagine her looking great in just about anything. She was tastefully casual and uncommonly attractive.

"Ever ridden on a motorcycle?" Valerie asked.

Jackie hesitated for a moment before shaking her head. She went to the window and peeked through the drapes. "Is that a Harley? It's beautiful!" The white motorcycle, majestic and intimidating, looked absolutely huge in the driveway.

"You might need a light jacket," Valerie said. "The ride back will be chilly."

Jackie went to the hall closet and found a windbreaker, still surprised at how excited she was. "Where are we going?"

"Do you like Thai food? I've heard good things about a new place not far from here."

In the driveway Valerie gave her a helmet and helped her put it on. Cool, nimble fingers touched Jackie's skin as she snapped the chin strap in place. They looked at each other, and Jackie noticed the gold flecks in Valerie's eyes. The mutual attraction had never been her imagination. There was more than a flicker of interest passing back and forth between them.

"You can hold on here," Valerie said, indicating a place on the seat, "or you can hold on to me, whichever makes you more comfortable."

"I take it this isn't your first time out, right?" Jackie said. "You know what you're doing on this thing?"

Valerie offered that very engaging smile of hers. "I've been around the block a few times."

Jackie chuckled and then mumbled under her breath, "I bet you have." She climbed on the motorcycle, assuming that she'd feel better not touching Valerie at all and holding the sides of the seat, but once they were off and rumbling down the street, it was the most natural thing in the world to hold on to Valerie's waist.

"You okay?" Valerie shouted behind her after they'd traveled a ways and stopped at a red light.

"Yes!" They were at the restaurant much too quickly as far as Jackie was concerned. She had truly enjoyed the ride.

The food was excellent, and they stayed there afterward talking and drinking coffee. "So how are things really at the office?" Valerie asked. "Buzz left me a message, but I haven't called him back yet."

"He's pretty disappointed," Jackie said. "You made things easier for a while, and now you're gone. I'm sure he wants to know why."

"Buzz has probably figured it out by now," she said quietly. "He knows how attracted I am to you, but he was hoping it would blow over."

Jackie leaned back in the booth and studied her for a moment. Their eyes met again, and Jackie willed herself not to get distracted by Valerie's full, sensual lips. "The two of you have discussed this?"

"He's very perceptive." Valerie held the look, and Jackie felt light-headed for a moment. "And he's very protective of you," she added.

Jackie toyed with the spoon on her saucer.

"So, Ms. Knovac," Valerie said with a smile. "What does it take to impress you?"

Jackie shrugged. "That's a very nice motorcycle you've got there."

"I didn't wear my black leather jacket. I wasn't sure you'd be ready for that."

The thought of her in leather brought an unexpected shiver to Jackie's entire body. She rubbed her arms to help smooth the bumps away. They talked about D.J. and the repairs to the house. Valerie relayed several amusing stories about D.J.'s exploits during the one semester of college they'd spent together. The remainder of the evening was full of generic chatter and easy laughter.

The ride back to her house was indeed much cooler, but Jackie just leaned a little closer than she had before. Valerie's body was warm and sweet smelling, and Jackie had to admit that she couldn't remember the last time she'd had so much fun.

"Come in and warm up," Jackie said after climbing off the Harley. She unlocked the door and held it open. "How about a cappuccino? I've got this great cappuccino maker I haven't used in a while."

In the kitchen, Jackie turned on lights and motioned toward the table. It seemed strange having someone new in the house. Jackie had never thought of this place as home, so they were both strangers in these surroundings. Her father had bought it a few years before he died.

A while later, Valerie cleaned the remnants of a white foamy mustache off her upper lip with the tip of her tongue. "I have two Melissa Etheridge tickets for Saturday night. Would you like to go?"

Jackie wondered briefly who the tickets had originally been purchased for since the concert had been sold out for weeks, but she didn't dwell on it long. She laughed suddenly. "Could we go on the Harley?"

"Sure. Unless it rains." Valerie tossed her hair away from her face. "I want you to know that I'm not seeing anyone else right now."

Their eyes met across the table, and Jackie could feel herself tensing up and getting nervous. "And it's only fair that you know that it wouldn't make any difference to me if you were." Jackie picked up their empty cups and set them in the sink. "We went to dinner, and we're going to a concert. Let's keep it as simple as that."

Valerie smiled and nodded.

Christ, you're young, Jackie thought. *Gorgeous, but young.*

"You aren't going to make this easy for me, are you?" Valerie said.

"I don't need anything complicating my life right now." Jackie led the way out of the kitchen and turned the porch light on from the hallway. "With me trying to get this house ready to sell and then having a very capable assistant quit at the office, I don't have time for anything else."

"A little diversion every now and then can be healthy."

Jackie smiled. "Is that what you are? A little diversion?"

"If you feel comfortable thinking of me that way, then I'd love to be your little diversion."

Jackie opened the door and leaned against it. "I'm not looking for anything, Valerie. Just remember that." They walked outside together, and Jackie watched her gracefully climb back on the motorcycle and then bring it to life before roaring off into the night. It had been a nice, nonthreatening evening.

During the three days between their dinner date on Tuesday and the concert on Saturday, Jackie and Valerie spoke on the phone for a total of three hours. Valerie was out of town visiting relatives and usually called just as things were beginning to wind down for the night. Jackie had been putting in some seriously long hours at the office, and when she got home every night she either had to finish up some last-minute work on her computer or help D.J. with one of many two-people projects left to do around the house.

Friday night after turning her computer off and catching a quick shower, Jackie took the phone to bed with her and waited for Valerie's call. She forced herself to let it ring twice before answering it. She didn't want to appear too eager.

Saturday morning Jackie slept in and wanted to be rested for the concert. D.J. had made coffee already and had left a catalog of outdoor plants for her perusal under the stack of receipts.

A while later D.J. came in the back door. "Anything in there catch your eye?" she asked as she nodded toward the catalog.

"I'm getting this place fixed up to sell," Jackie reminded her again. "It's not like I'll be living here for the rest of my life." She looked up at her and handed over the catalog. "Maybe the new owners will have a mind of their own and want a whole different type of landscaping."

"Yeah, maybe." D.J. poured another cup of coffee. "But houses usually sell better when you have live shrubs in the yard."

Jackie took the catalog back and smacked her playfully on the arm with it. "Wouldn't it be cheaper to just get some green paint and spray all the dead stuff with it?" she suggested. "You're really obsessed with this live plant thing, aren't you?"

D.J. rolled her eyes. "The pool," she said. "Are you fixing the pool?"

"That depends. How much do you know about pools?"

"Zip, but I know they're not supposed to have things growing in them. I've got a friend who can probably help. You want an estimate?"

Saturday night it rained, so Jackie and Valerie went to dinner and then the concert in Valerie's candy-apple-red Miata convertible.

"You've certainly got nice wheels for someone without a job," Jackie noted.

Valerie laughed. "You think so? I've got two interviews next week."

The theater had wall-to-wall lesbians and promised to be a reaffirming experience. Melissa Etheridge T-shirts, programs, and trinkets could be seen everywhere, and the crowd was almost as entertaining as the concert itself.

Afterward they stopped at a coffee shop for a late-night snack and sat talking for another two hours. On the way home Jackie wanted the top down since it had stopped raining.

"This is great," she yelled as they zoomed through traffic with wind caressing their faces.

"What are you doing tomorrow?" Valerie asked. She looked down at her watch and then corrected herself. "I mean today. What are you doing today?"

"Is it today already?" Jackie asked. Her eyes were closed and she could feel her hair whipping around her head. She felt free and frivolous, and she never wanted the car or the wind to stop. Jackie turned her head in Valerie's direction and asked, "Would you teach me how to drive the Harley?" Valerie's profile made Jackie's heart beat a little faster. Her tanned face with its delicate jaw and perfect nose. Valerie's eyes seemed to twinkle when she smiled, and her laughter was almost contagious at times.

"Do you drive or ride a motorcycle?" Jackie asked after a moment. "Which is it?"

"You ride," Valerie said. "You wouldn't drive a bicycle, would you?"

"No, I guess not. Then teach me how to ride the Harley. Could we do that tomorrow?"

The next day Valerie was once again punctual, and she even arrived bearing a gift. "If you're gonna do this, then let's do it right. Turn around. We're about the same size." She helped Jackie put the black leather jacket on. "I've got a closetful of these. You can have this one." Valerie took her by the shoulders and turned an amazed Jackie around before nodding her approval. "Now you're ready."

Jackie unconsciously played with the zippers and ran her hands over the cool, smooth surface. She studied her reflection in the hall mirror and was speechless. There was something elegantly butch about wearing a jacket like this. The transformation excited her. Jackie wasn't sure she would ever want to take it off.

Valerie headed for the lake, stating that she knew where a few seldom-used maintenance roads were. She explained that she didn't want Jackie learning to ride in traffic. An hour later she stopped in the middle of a deserted road and got off the Harley.

"My father taught me to ride when I was fourteen," she said, "so don't get nervous. Anybody can do this."

The clutch was the tricky part, but thirty minutes after her first lesson, Jackie was riding and in total control of the monstrous machine. Valerie was very patient about giving instructions, and Jackie noticed right away that having Valerie's body pressing against her back was almost as thrilling as opening up the throttle.

A while later they watched the sun go down from a ridge overlooking the lake. Jackie was once again a passenger, and even when the Harley wasn't moving, she kept her arms around Valerie's waist. She would never forget the way Valerie's jacket felt in her hands as she held on to her, or the way Valerie occasionally leaned back, pressing firmly against her breasts.

Later, in Jackie's driveway, they took their helmets off and set them on the seat. Jackie suggested a cappuccino for the road and led the way up the sidewalk to the house.

"We got a little sun today," Jackie said as she spied her reflection in the hall mirror.

Valerie stepped up behind her and looked at both of their sunburned faces. "Helmet hair is very becoming on you."

"Hmm." It was the first personal remark Jackie had heard from her in days, and hearing it wasn't nearly as unsettling as it once would've been.

Jackie recognized the laughter coming from the backyard and took a chance on catching naked lovers outside. She invited the fully-clothed but slightly rumpled Carla and D.J. in for a cappuccino after getting their attention. Carla's pop-eyed look when she saw Valerie at the table almost made Jackie laugh. They hadn't chatted much since things had got so hot with D.J. Forty-five minutes later when everyone was leaving, Carla leaned over and whispered, "We'll talk tomorrow, you sneaky shit."

Out in the driveway Jackie rubbed her hand over the Harley's fine leather seat. She fastened the extra helmet down securely and watched as Valerie climbed back on the bike. Her long legs, so shapely and tempting as they held the motorcycle up, would undoubtedly be a traffic hazard to anyone getting a glimpse of her. If the Harley itself didn't draw its share of attention, then its rider would surely have admirers of her own.

"Be careful going home," Jackie said. "And thanks for the jacket."

"My pleasure. Can we have dinner tomorrow?"

Jackie smiled. "I don't know. Work's been tough since you left. I might get stuck at the office late."

"You still have to eat," Valerie reminded her as she started the motorcycle. "I'll call you." She backed up the bike, her black boots sliding on the pavement as she moved. Roaring off into the night, she left Jackie with a sense of regret at having let her go. It had been another nice, nonthreatening evening.

They had a late dinner on Monday and celebrated Valerie's new job. "I was the only one they wanted to interview."

"When do you start?"

"Monday." Valerie laughed. "It gives me all week to play."

"I haven't played in so long I'm not sure I'd remember how." Jackie looked across the table at the candlelight dancing in Valerie's eyes. Her hair was a fine cloud of layered curls, and her lips were a glossy pink almost begging to be kissed. Jackie had a sudden, overwhelming desire to touch her and was terrified to really admit it.

"Fiesta starts this weekend," Valerie said. "Would you like to go?"

"I'm busy this weekend," Jackie said, having no idea where it came from. She set her tea glass down as soon as she noticed her hand shaking.

Valerie asked for the check, and they both forked over money, something they'd agreed on the first time they had gone out together.

"Can we drive with the top down?" Jackie asked when they'd reached Valerie's car. She wanted the wind in her face again and thoughts out of her head. *You're beginning to like her too much, Knovac. Here you are breaking your own rules.* Jackie rested her head on the back of the seat and closed her eyes. She would miss this cute little fast car. No doubt about it.

In Jackie's driveway, they got out and put the Miata's top back up. "Do I get a cappuccino for the road?" Valerie asked.

Jackie unlocked the front door and tossed her keys on the small table in the hallway. Valerie's hand touched her arm, and Jackie turned around.

"Can we talk for a minute?" Valerie asked and nodded toward the living room. Jackie turned a lamp on and chose to sit in the rocker across from the sofa. She watched as Valerie moved pillows back and forth and got comfortable.

"I can feel you pulling away from me," Valerie said. Her beige turtleneck fit her perfectly and made her breasts seem so inviting, inviting enough that Jackie had to look somewhere else. Valerie tossed another small pillow aside and draped her arm along the back of the sofa. "Being patient isn't nearly as easy as I thought it would be. I want you so much that I can't think about anything else."

Jackie's heart began to race. She met Valerie's serious, searching eyes and then got up and went to the fireplace. "You know nothing about me," Jackie whispered huskily.

"I know all I need to know."

Valerie was behind her—that hint of perfume still as intoxicating as ever. Valerie turned her around and grazed the side of Jackie's face with a fingertip, her eyes once again slowly searching Jackie's.

"I stay awake at night thinking about you," Valerie said, "and then when I finally do fall asleep I have the most wonderful, erotic dreams. Sometimes I hope I'll never wake up if that's the only way I can have you."

She moved her hand to the back of Jackie's head and gently pulled her closer. Her mouth was on Jackie's, and they instantly melted into each other with hot, searing passion.

"Oh, God," Jackie breathed. Not only was she allowing this to happen, but she realized that she wanted it as much as Valerie did. She tilted her head back and encouraged Valerie's mouth on her throat.

"Such vivid erotic dreams about you," Valerie whispered. "So far I've made love to you twice on a motorcycle and once on the table in the conference room at the office."

"Twice on a motorcycle?" The thought excited her. Jackie found Valerie's mouth again and felt her tremble with unadulterated desire. Jackie's hands were under Valerie's sweater, and Jackie was delighted to discover that Valerie wasn't wearing a bra. As her fingers danced over warm soft skin, one thought kept fluttering inside Jackie's head—*She quit her job for you, Knovac. No one has ever wanted you this much.*

Chapter Five

Very little momentum was lost on the way up the stairs. Once inside Jackie's bedroom, they were all over each other again. It was dark except for a sliver of moonlight slicing through the broken slats in the blinds. Jackie found the rustling of clothing, the fumbling of buttons, and the sound of zippers inching down just as exciting as having Valerie's tongue in her mouth. She could hear little moans escaping from her own throat each time Valerie touched her, and Valerie's talented hands were absolutely everywhere.

Jackie couldn't remember the last time someone had made love to her and actually meant it. An orgasm had never been a given for her—each one was always a treasured surprise. But this time was different. Jackie's body was hot, pulsating, and she knew right away that she would come with this woman.

Valerie tugged the shirttail from Jackie's pants and moved the shirt away to kiss her bare shoulder. She made a trail with her tongue back to the soft hollow of her throat as clothes began surrounding them in little piles on the floor. Jackie kissed her again and led her to the bed where their naked bodies finally merged completely. Valerie reached for her and rubbed slowly through crisp curls before slipping two fingers inside.

"God, you're so wet," Valerie said. She rolled Jackie over on her back, keeping her fingers in place, moving them slowly in and out. She took a hard nipple in her mouth, and Jackie arched her back and encouraged her to take more.

Gone was the apprehension that Jackie had always felt during sex with Phyllis. And gone was the indifference Jackie remembered seeing in Karen's eyes each time they'd made love their first year together. Occasionally Jackie wondered if during those last few months before Karen died, when she was secretly sleeping with someone else, if Karen's new lover had ever seen that dull emptiness in her expression.

But this, Jackie thought, *this Valerie Dennison is something new.* Being pursued and courted instead of stalked and lied to. Being pampered and teased instead of smacked and used. Valerie was an experience Jackie was looking forward to.

She wanted to feel her, and managed to work a knee in between Valerie's long, shapely legs. Valerie gasped and slowly began moving against her—sliding and grinding herself into Jackie's thigh. The room was cool, but they were both beginning to sweat, and Jackie absolutely *adored* sweaty sex.

She ran her tongue along the side of Valerie's swaying breasts. Just taking a nipple in her mouth started the roller coaster tumbling in the pit of her stomach. Valerie made a wonderful moaning sound and began moving more vigorously against Jackie's wet thigh. Fingers were still inside of her, when Jackie was as close to coming as Valerie was. They were a shuddering mass of arms and legs, both crying out their pleasure as they moved. Valerie buried her face in Jackie's neck, kissing her and murmuring a string of endearments. They stayed that way for a long time, and Jackie was reminded once again why this was one of her favorite things about making love—that moment after when words weren't necessary.

"That was fabulous," Valerie finally whispered. Her breathing was beginning to return to normal, but she was still firmly attached to Jackie's thigh. "I don't think I'm ready to move yet."

"That's fine with me," Jackie said, and smoothed the hair away from her face. "You're even more beautiful in the throes of passion."

"And that's exactly where I've been," she said into Jackie's neck. Her voice was husky and muffled. *Holding her is wonderful,* Jackie thought. *What made me think I could do without this?*

Jackie raised her knee up a little and smiled at Valerie's reaction. "Getting naked and sweaty with a coworker wouldn't have been nearly as much fun," Jackie noted.

Valerie kissed her gently on the lips and then reluctantly disengaged herself from Jackie's leg. "If I'd known this was a possibility, I'd have quit that job the first day." Valerie stretched out beside her and propped her head up with her hand. Her silly grin was contagious. "I think I've recovered enough now to give you the attention you deserve." Her finger made a trail from Jackie's chin on down to her navel. "I'd like to kiss you everywhere," she said as she leaned over and touched the tip of her tongue to Jackie's hard, quivering nipple, "and then I'd like to taste you here," she murmured as fingers lightly danced through moist curls. "And then I'd like to lick you and suck you until you beg me to stop."

Jackie laughed. "Weeks later they'll find you still buried between my legs."

"Mmm. I should be so lucky."

Jackie woke up to delicious, titillating stimulation and was aware from the deep well of sleep that her thighs were being gently urged apart. The lump under the cover at three in the morning kissed her way up Jackie's leg, bare breasts hovering over her shins, grazing Jackie's knee. Valerie's fingers aroused as well as parted her, and Valerie's nose slowly teased her as she rubbed it up and down over Jackie's swollen center. As promised earlier, Valerie's tongue and lips finally woke her completely, and she indeed sucked and licked every part of her until Jackie was much too weak to beg her to stop.

Afterward Valerie kissed the inside of Jackie's thigh and crawled farther up under the covers. Valerie laid her head on Jackie's shoulder and fell asleep in her arms almost instantly, but before drifting off to sleep again Valerie had mumbled something that had sounded like, "I needed a snack."

As daylight crept into the room, Jackie's dreams were peaceful, and memories of the night before made her smile. A while later she squinted in the direction of the alarm clock and knew there was no way she could get to work on time.

There was nothing urgent waiting for her at the office today, but she still needed to get there at a reasonable hour.

She propped her pillow up and watched Valerie sleep—a spray of light brown curls covered her forehead; full pink lips were slightly parted. Jackie leaned over and kissed her before shuffling off to the shower. She didn't care to think about the will-she-want-to-stay-again-tonight question. Once Jackie allowed herself to feel something for someone, a whole new person was known to emerge, and Jackie wasn't sure she was ready for any of that right now.

She heard a toilet flush, and then a few moments later she heard a voice still husky from sleep.

"Room for two in there?" Valerie called.

Jackie opened the shower door with a soapy hand. They kissed under the spray with one hot, continuous exchange of tongues. Jackie couldn't believe how quickly this woman's mouth could excite her. Just a kiss turned her to jelly. She'd definitely be late for work now.

Water washed the soap and all remnants of shampoo from their bodies as they held each other. Valerie's hand moved from Jackie's breast to between her legs.

"You're so wet," Valerie said, and then chuckled. She kissed her way up to Jackie's ear and licked the water dripping from the lobe. "God, I want you." Fingers slipped inside of her and began a gentle stroking. "Last night," Valerie whispered. "Last night you tasted so good."

"I can't do this standing up," Jackie said breathlessly. She felt like a rag doll, limp and submissive.

"Sure you can," Valerie whispered. Her fingers moved with precision and determination as she held her up with her other arm. "Come for me."

Her lips found Jackie's again, and that extraordinary tongue began another surge of magic as she probed the very core of Jackie's existence. Jackie pulled her mouth away and draped her arms around Valerie's neck. She tilted her head back and let the water hit her face. The heat between her legs began to spread up her stomach; Valerie's lips again tugged on her ear. She kissed Jackie's wet throat and shoulder, and Jackie trembled when Valerie once again whispered, "Come for me."

Jackie tightened her arms around her neck and let Valerie hold her up. "Faster," Jackie said. *Oh, Jesus, this feels good!* "Hold me . . . please . . . hold me. Oh, God. Don't stop . . ." Jackie came and threw her head back again. She rode Valerie's fingers until every last ounce of pleasure was drained from her body. Shaking and breathless, she whispered urgently, "Hold me."

"I am," Valerie said. "God, you're beautiful."

Jackie kept her arms around Valerie's neck until that Jell-O feeling left her legs. Valerie slowly pulled her fingers from her and kissed her again.

Jackie went downstairs to the smell of fresh coffee and stood in the doorway to the kitchen buttoning the sleeves of her white blouse. She found Valerie and D.J. deep in conversation across the kitchen, both with steaming cups of coffee in hand. D.J. leaned against the back door and raised her cup in Jackie's direction in a good-morning salute. Valerie handed Jackie her very own cup of coffee, already fixed the way she liked it, and looked over at her with a smile.

"What's on the agenda today?" Jackie asked no one in particular. She glanced at the coffeepot to see if any receipts had been left.

"Planting your buffalo grass and getting an estimate on the pool." D.J. opened the back door. "And I need to get started on it while it's cool. See you later."

Valerie set her cup down and stepped into Jackie's arms. The ends of her hair were still damp from the shower. "What's on your agenda today, Ms. Knovac?" She straightened the collar of Jackie's blouse.

"Work. There's another briefing on the Flanagan account this afternoon." Jackie closed her eyes as Valerie's finger traced a slow line down the side of her face and stopped at the corner of her mouth.

"I have plans for you tonight," Valerie whispered. Her eyes were the color of maple with flecks of gold visible in the light from the kitchen. Jackie felt captured in the gaze. The fluttering in her stomach unnerved her a little, but there was still an overwhelming urge to pull this woman into her arms again.

"You're late for work," Valerie said. She moved back away from her, tossing the mane of hair from her face. "I'll call you later."

Jackie watched her leave and then heard the front door close. She slowly let out the deep breath she'd been holding and leaned back against the counter. *Valerie Dennison has some serious potential. Very serious potential.*

At work Jackie stayed busy, but not busy enough to keep from thinking about the night before and the morning after. Several times during the day she wanted to hear Valerie's voice, wanted to remind herself that she hadn't imagined any of this. The passion Valerie invoked and the understanding she seemed to have for Jackie's needs was a little overwhelming, but Jackie was at a point in her life where being overwhelmed was a blessing.

She glanced at the telephone on her desk and realized again that she didn't know how to get in touch with her. She was almost certain that Valerie wouldn't call her at the office, and that made for an even longer day.

At home that evening, Jackie unlocked the door and took her heels off almost before setting her briefcase down. She turned on lights everywhere and checked her answering machine. The last message was from Valerie stating that she'd be there at seven with a Chinese takeout feast. Jackie glanced at her watch and decided she had enough time for a quick shower. It had been a long, tedious day at the office.

At seven sharp Jackie answered the door. Valerie whizzed in, loaded down with several white bags and a bottle of plum wine tucked under her arm.

"I brought a little bit of everything," she said.

Jackie followed her to the kitchen, admiring the fit of her tight jeans. Even covered in denim, Valerie's legs were causing a flutter or two.

Arms went around her waist as Jackie reached for plates in the cabinet, and soft full breasts were snug against her back. Jackie set the plates on the counter and closed her eyes as Valerie's warm, sweet breath touched her neck.

"I spent all day thinking about you," Valerie whispered. Her hands slid up and cupped Jackie's breasts. "How hungry are you?"

Lips brushed Jackie's ear, and Valerie's tongue started a cool, slow caress along its edge. One hand moved down to the top of her pants and eased a smooth palm inside.

Again Valerie whispered, "How hungry are you?"

Jackie answered her by tilting her head back and finding Valerie's mouth. Food couldn't have been farther from her mind as Valerie's tongue met hers. The kiss was deep and intoxicating, and those soft lips seeking more, demanding more, had Jackie trembling within seconds.

Jackie had a weak spot for good kissers, and Valerie undoubtedly excelled in this area. If Valerie had done nothing more than kiss her, it would've been enough, but she didn't stop there. She could tease with her mouth and bring Jackie close to the edge. Her hand under Jackie's shirt was nice, and that same hand easing a zipper down and slipping inside the band of her underwear was indeed an added bonus. Jackie felt her jeans being loosed at her hips and her shirt being opened to free her breasts. Valerie took that exquisite mouth away to cover a nipple.

"No," Jackie gasped. "Kiss me, goddamn it." She filled her hands with Valerie's hair and pulled her head back up to search for her mouth again. "Kiss me," Jackie whispered urgently. "Kiss me."

How Jackie eventually ended up on the table was a mystery. Valerie kissed her in a feverish show of desire. And Valerie's fluttering fingers between Jackie's legs threatened to take her breath away. Valerie's hot, insistent tongue probed Jackie's mouth and brought her closer to oblivion each time Valerie touched her.

Valerie pulled her mouth away and kissed the side of Jackie's face as fingers continued gliding between her legs.

"I want my tongue inside you," Valerie said in a husky whisper. "I need to taste you again."

Jackie's hands were in her hair, urging her downward, suggesting, but only briefly. Valerie apparently needed no further encouragement.

PART II
Valerie

Chapter Six

Valerie scanned the crowded restaurant for Benny's table and finally noticed his napkin waving in the air like a flag of surrender. He pulled a chair out for her and kissed her on the cheek.

"You always look so butch in a three-piece suit," she teased.

"Thank you," he replied in mock seriousness. "I've been told I need all the help I can get."

Benjamin E. Tackett III was Valerie's best friend. Having known each other since they were toddlers when their grandfathers had become business partners, they were closer than most siblings. During the mid-Fifties, the Dennisons and the Tacketts had formed Dentac, an advertising agency with an impressive reputation in state, national, and international arenas. It was a multimillion-dollar business that had left Valerie and Benny very wealthy before either had reached puberty. Benny was currently being groomed by his father, Benjamin E. Tackett Jr., for a vice president position. This career move kept Benny in the closet for a number of reasons, two of which involved remaining on his parents' good side as well as attempting to comply with the stipulations of his grandfather's will.

In order for Benny to receive the bulk of his twenty-million-dollar estate on his thirtieth birthday, Benjamin E. Tackett Sr., Benny's grandfather, had made it quite clear before he died that his grandson had to marry. Benny loved his grandfather dearly but surmised that the old man had probably sensed something a bit "unnatural" about him at a very young age. And how better to get Benny's attention and spur him on to a more "normal" path than money?

It was with this in mind that Benny chose to get married the summer before his grandfather died. After the ceremony, everyone in the church had let loose with a collective sigh of relief. His family was unaware, however, that Colin, Benny's lover, had served as his best man and would be accompanying the newlyweds on the honeymoon. Benny Tackett could play their game for twenty million, and so far he had succeeded in squelching any doubts about his commitment to heterosexuality.

Valerie closed her menu and made her selection for lunch. With the waiter on his way to place their orders, Benny then gave her a questioning, easy look.

"Well?" he said. "Colin sent me here with explicit instructions about finding out where you've been for two weekends in a row."

Valerie eyed him with a smirk and sipped her water. "I'm seeing someone."

He smiled, showing off his perfect white teeth. "Will we approve? When do we get to meet her?"

Valerie laughed and shook out her napkin. "I don't care if you approve or not."

"Oh," he said, surprised. "This is serious." He reached over and gave her hand a squeeze. "Good for you. It's about time." The waiter brought their iced tea and salads. "Who is she? Tell me about her."

Valerie smiled as she thought about Jackie—that demure, no-nonsense persona on the outside and the passionate amusing woman on the inside. Valerie knew how vulnerable Jackie was right now and hoped eventually to gain her trust. She hated the way old lovers occasionally made it so much harder for the new lover. Every relationship came with its own baggage, some good and some bad. The bad, however, always seemed to arrive on time no matter what the circumstances were or how hard the new lover tried to get rid of it.

"I worked for her at my last job," Valerie said. "She's also a friend of D.J.'s."

Benny glanced at her with a raised eyebrow. He had that Clark Kent look—finely chiseled features, dark brown hair, and a six-foot-two frame. He was quite attractive in heels and a dress too. As teenagers they'd tried on each other's clothes occasionally. Benny had actually taught Valerie how to use makeup when they were kids.

"How is D.J.?" he asked. "I haven't seen her since New Year's."

"She's the same. Still doing what she wants when she wants."

Benny set his glass down and shook his head. He looked at her steadily for a moment. "You don't sound like a woman in love. What's up?"

Valerie shrugged. "How would you know what a woman in love sounds like?" She glanced at her watch. She only had an hour for lunch, and stretching the rules the first week on a new job didn't seem like a wise move. "Besides," she said as she set her glass aside to make room for her arriving plate, "I'm in love with her, but at this point she hasn't said whether or not she's in love with me yet."

"Oh."

"Then there's this Magda thing." She noticed how he paled at the mere mention of his mother, Magda Tackett. Magda worked out of Austin and ran the Dentac Agency there. She was famous for popping into town unannounced.

"I'm sorry," he said quietly. "I'll do whatever I can to—"

"I know," Valerie said with a wave of her hand. They both let the subject drop. "I'll handle this. It'll just take some time."

"Does this new woman in your life have a name?" Benny asked after a moment.

"Jackie Knovac." Valerie laughed nervously. Just saying Jackie's name made her head feel light. "She's a little older than I am."

"I always enjoyed having a lover who could teach me something." He smiled and blew on a forkful of quiche. "Before Colin, of course."

They shared a dessert and made plans for lunch again later in the week. Benny walked with her to her car and gave her a hug.

"Call us when you're free," he said. "Colin wants to have dinner with you soon."

Valerie nodded and promised to work them into her busy schedule.

D.J. and Carla were leaving just as Valerie pulled into Jackie's driveway that afternoon. They waved and made lewd whistling noises as she got out of the car. Valerie had left straight from work, fully clothed in her corporate drag—pale gray skirt and jacket with a lacy white blouse and matching gray heels. She draped a garment bag over her arm when she got out of the car.

"Hey, Mama!" D.J. called out the rolled-down window. "How much you charge?" They sped off to high-pitched laughter when Valerie waved her favorite finger at them.

Jackie was home from work already and had a nice dinner simmering away. Valerie hung her clothes in the hall closet before slipping into Jackie's arms. They kissed slowly, ardently, with Jackie's lips coming to Valerie's throat and ear before finding her mouth again.

"It's the bed or nothing tonight," Jackie whispered. "I can't be humping and thumping on floors and tables any more. I'm too old for that."

"Then the bed it is," Valerie said. She chuckled at the memory of how many places in the house they had made love already. Occasionally they tried the bed first, but passion seemed to consume them at the strangest times and places.

"Change clothes," Jackie said as she rubbed Valerie's butt through the soft fabric of her skirt. "Dinner's almost ready."

A while later over dinner, Jackie told her about getting complete control of the Flanagan account.

"That's a promotion," Valerie said flatly. At Jackie's nod, Valerie let out a screech and jumped up to kiss her. "This is great! How long have you worked for this?"

"Five years." Jackie raised her cup in a toast. "Buzz got my old job, and his new assistant got his." Jackie eyed her with a stern expression. "And if you had stayed, you would've gotten a promotion today as well, young lady."

Valerie turned in her chair and propped an elbow on the back in a seductive pose. "If I had stayed," she said simply, "I wouldn't have got the chance to do any humping and thumping with you, now would I, Ms. Knovac?"

Jackie blushed before laughing. "Yes. I suppose that's true." She finished her coffee and set the cup beside her empty plate. They cleaned off the table and loaded up the dishwasher. Valerie moved behind her and kissed Jackie's neck.

"Can we go to bed and talk?" Jackie asked quietly.

"Sure." Valerie took her by the hand and led the way upstairs. "With clothes on or off?"

"On," Jackie said. "Yes, definitely on. I talk much better with my clothes on."

"Me, too." Valerie moved to the center of the neatly made bed and patted the place beside her. Jackie pursed her lips and then shook her head.

"On second thought, we can't talk here." She turned abruptly and started for the bedroom door. "Downstairs."

Valerie followed her down the stairs and into the living room where she found Jackie sitting in the huge rocker near the fireplace. Valerie curled up on the sofa across from her and watched as Jackie drummed fingertips on the chair's wooden arms.

"What's going on?" Valerie finally whispered.

The drumming stopped, but then Jackie slowly began to rock.

"I wanted to call you today and tell you about my promotion," she said. She met Valerie's eyes and then cleared her throat before looking away again. "I realized that I didn't have a phone number for you. I don't know where you live or who your friends are. We've been seeing each other for weeks now. Why don't I know more about you? How could I let this happen?" She continued rocking slowly and staring at the coffee table between them.

"What exactly are you upset about?" Valerie asked.

"I don't even know," Jackie admitted wearily. She sighed and then met Valerie's eyes again. "I think I freaked out a little when I went looking for your phone number. It hit me that I'd never called you before. You've always called me."

"You've never seemed interested in calling me before," Valerie said.

"Is that what you think?"

"Isn't it true? I've always initiated any contact we have. You seemed more comfortable with that." Valerie got up and put her hands on the arms of the rocker, leaning in close to her. "This is good," she whispered. "Don't be afraid to need me."

Jackie smiled reluctantly. "You think you know me pretty well, don't you?"

"Not at all. You're still full of surprises. And if you're really wondering about where I live, we could go there right now. I'll give you a tour. Would you like that?" She took

Jackie's hands and pulled her up. Her lips brushed just below Jackie's ear.

"It's too far," Jackie whispered. "Wherever you live is too far." Valerie led her to the sofa and continued kissing her throat and shoulder. "Your new job," Jackie said with some difficulty. "How many women work there with you?"

"Three."

"Younger or older than you?"

Valerie laughed softly and ran the tip of her tongue along Jackie's ear. "All three are older than me."

"Are they married or single?"

"One married and two are divorced."

Jackie slipped a hand inside Valerie's shirt. "Do you work directly for any of them?"

"Directly? No. Why are you asking me these things?" With a fingertip under Jackie's chin, Valerie tilted her head up a little. All caressing had stopped. "Are you insinuating that I'm attracted to the women I work for?"

"I'm not insinuating anything," Jackie said. "I'm interested in what your coworkers are like. You never talk about them. Actually, you never really talk about anything."

"It's never seemed important before."

"Maybe that's my fault," Jackie said. "We only focus on one thing when we're together now." She resumed her search inside Valerie's shirt.

"That might be true for you." Valerie wanted to take her in her arms and tell her how much she loved her, but something was holding her back. She sensed that Jackie was looking for an excuse to minimize how they related to one another. This was more than sex for Valerie, and she wanted it to be more than sex for Jackie, too.

"My age bothers you, doesn't it?" Valerie said.

Jackie laughed uneasily. "Only when I think about it."

Valerie trailed a finger along the edge of her mouth. "Then don't think about it. The older we get, the less it'll matter."

"Why don't you play with women your own age?" Jackie whispered.

"They're so boring." Valerie pulled her closer and kissed her. "If they can't tell me what they were doing the day Kennedy was shot, then I'm not interested."

Jackie gently pushed her back on the sofa and worked a knee in between Valerie's legs. "You weren't even born when Kennedy was shot." She covered Valerie's mouth with her own and Valerie felt the heat quickly spreading through her whole body.

"We're humping and thumping on the furniture again," Valerie whispered before nuzzling Jackie's sweet-smelling neck. Jackie chuckled but didn't stop until they were both ragged and sweaty.

Valerie met Colin in the hallway outside of her apartment. She could tell by the quickness of his step that he needed something urgently.

"Valerie, dear. Please tell me you have oregano." Colin nudged a stray lock of wavy red hair away from his brow and took both of the full shopping bags from her. "This sauce is just screaming for it, and I've searched those cabinets from top to bottom. The kitchen's a wreck," he said. He rearranged the bags in his arms before mumbling, "I think I panicked a bit. Like a drag queen looking for lost eyeliner, I tell you."

Valerie laughed and opened the door. "Check the cabinet by the sink." She took one of the bags from him and set it on the counter. "Where's Benny?"

"Golfing with Junior," Colin said.

Valerie laughed again. Benjamin E. Tackett Jr., Benny's father, liked being called Ben, but in private Colin always referred to him as Junior.

"What does Benny know about golf?" Valerie asked.

"He says that miniature putt-putt stuff's a whiz, so how hard can the real thing be? Same ball, just more clubs to choose from." Colin peeked in each grocery bag. "He went out and took three emergency lessons this week so he wouldn't embarrass himself. Bought new clothes and everything."

"When is he going to get a real job, Colin?"

It was Colin's turn to laugh. "Benny hates to work! This is perfect for him." He picked up the bottle of oregano and kissed her on the cheek. "Come over for dinner later and hear all about his golfing debut."

"I've got plans already."

Colin leaned against the counter and tilted his head back to get a better look at her. "What kind of plans? Benny mentioned that you were seeing someone." He took the milk out of a bag and put it in the refrigerator for her.

"I'm staying over at her place tonight," Valerie said.

"Oh, we'll have to do dinner soon," Colin cooed. "We want to hear all about this. When can we meet her?"

Valerie snatched three tomatoes from him just before he started to juggle them. "Not until she's ready. You two will take some explaining, and I'm too busy to have to explain anything right now."

Colin wagged a finger in her face. "Don't forget to tell her about Magda. You should get that all taken care of right away."

Just the mere mention of Magda's name made them both instantly depressed. Valerie put her elbows on the counter next to him, with both of them remaining that way for the longest time. Finally Colin said, "Maybe she'll stay in Austin for good."

"Yeah, maybe."

Chapter Seven

D.J., Carla, Valerie, and Jackie were out by Jackie's newly-repaired and recently-filled pool as steaks and ears of corn cooked on the grill. D.J. and Carla were floating on air mattresses, holding hands and sipping margaritas while Valerie and Jackie dangled their feet in the water from the pool's edge.

"Are you sure you want to sell this place?" Valerie asked. She looked around at the new grass and perky shrubs. The fence, house, and workshop had fresh paint, and the sidewalk leading to the garage and workshop was bone white in the late afternoon sun. The place was looking good.

"You're the second person who's asked me that."

Valerie leaned back and propped herself up with her arms. Jackie's foot rubbed along her calf in the water.

"Well?" Valerie prompted.

"Well what?" Jackie said. "It's close to work and there's plenty of room here, but I don't like this neighborhood. Since my ex-lover found me again, I've never really felt safe here."

"Then sell it," Valerie said just as her beeper went off. She tugged at the waistband of her shorts to check the number on the digital display. *Oh, shit! It's Benny!* "I need to use your phone."

They had agreed not to page each other for anything except a Magda emergency. Valerie grabbed a towel and dried her legs off at the back porch, and from the phone in the kitchen dialed the number. Benny answered on a half ring.

"Lunch in Austin tomorrow," he said. "Can you make it?"

"If it keeps her out of San Antonio," Valerie said, "then yeah, I can make it."

Benny let out a deep breath. "Bless you. We'll leave around ten. Thanks a million," he said, and laughed wearily at his own tired joke.

Valerie smiled, knowing how hard it must have been for him to call her on a Saturday afternoon. "I'll see you in the morning." She hung up just as Jackie came in.

"Everything okay?"

Valerie stuck her hands in her pockets. "I need to go out of town tomorrow. Please make me get out of here by eight in the morning."

"What's the occasion?"

"It's a family thing."

"Help me make a salad," Jackie said. "The steaks are almost done."

83

Valerie got a large bowl from the cabinet and took some fresh vegetables from the refrigerator.

"Tell me about your family," Jackie said. "You never talk about them. Do you have any siblings? Are you out to your parents?"

"I'm an only child, and I told them I was gay on my fourteenth birthday."

"Oh, dear," Jackie said. She pulled the head of lettuce apart and began washing it. "You've been at this a while, haven't you? How did they take it?"

"Good. About like I expected. I should probably interject here that my parents aren't ordinary people," Valerie said. "They were young hippies in the late sixties, and they're still liberal Democrats and avid environmentalists. They've got the usual SAVE THE WHALES and RIGHT TO CHOOSE bumper stickers on their cars. When I was a kid I was embarrassed to bring my friends over because my dad played his Janis Joplin albums so loud. When I was still in diapers I knew all the words to Down on Me."

"The lesbian national anthem," Jackie said with a hoot. "Go on."

"Needless to say, my friends were forever begging me to trade parents with them." Valerie shrugged and continued slicing tomato wedges. "By the time I was twenty I'd started to appreciate them more. They've been very supportive of me and my choices." Valerie smiled and glanced over at her. "They've been asking about you."

"Me?" Jackie shut the water off. "You told them about us?"

"Of course." Valerie laughed at the surprise on Jackie's face. She reached for a cucumber and rinsed it off. "They know I'm in love with you."

Jackie dropped her paring knife and gave them both a start. "You are?" She dried her hands on a paper towel and tossed it in the trash can by the pantry. "You told them before you told me?"

Valerie shrugged and began whittling on the cucumber. "I've told you in a hundred ways, but I guess you're not ready to listen yet." She finished the cucumber and reached for a bell pepper. "I can be very patient. One of these days you'll have to take me seriously."

Jackie's hand was on Valerie's arm, steady and firm, turning her around. They both jumped as the door opened.

"The steaks are done," Carla announced. "Get me a plate and I'll bring 'em in."

Jackie got the plate and followed Carla outside. D.J. came in and helped set the table, her baggy T-shirt hitting her at the knees and covering up her wet bathing suit. When Carla and Jackie didn't return with steaks and roasted ears of corn right away, D.J. went to the window by the sink.

"What are they doing?" Valerie asked. Her stomach was in knots. Had she blown it? Had she spoken too soon?

"They're talking by the grill," D.J. said. "At least the food's off the fire. What's going on?" She went to the back door and pulled it open. "Hey, you two! The salad's wilting! Hurry up."

A few minutes later Jackie and Carla came back in. Everyone sat down and filled their plates. Things seemed so normal for the first few minutes that Valerie began to relax again, but the knot returned when Jackie leaned over and asked, "When did you know?"

"When did I know what?"

"That you loved me."

Their voices were low. Carla and D.J. were deep into a conversation of their own about their preferences for either a margarita on the rocks or the frozen variety.

"I was immensely attracted to you the first day I saw you," Valerie said without embarrassment. Their eyes met, and Valerie recognized the serious don't-bullshit-me look that Jackie had perfected at work. "Even before the office gossip revealed your fondness for women," Valerie added. She stopped and took her time to think further before once again attempting to answer the question. "The night of the Melissa Etheridge concert," Valerie said. "The ride back in my car. I didn't want to take you home that night."

They had both stopped pretending to eat. Jackie turned in her chair, her arm resting on its high back.

"What is it you expect to get out of this?" Jackie asked.

Valerie felt a heaviness in her chest as those dark eyes searched her face. She took her napkin and tucked it beside her untouched plate.

"Just let me love you," Valerie said. "That's all I've ever wanted."

As they continued to look at one another, Valerie saw the tears forming in Jackie's eyes. She watched her slowly fold her napkin and set it on the table. Jackie pushed her chair away and was out the back door in a flash.

Valerie closed her eyes and smacked the table with her hand. "Fuck!"

"What the hell?" D.J. said as she steadied her margarita.

"Go after her," Carla said. She speared a cucumber with her fork and popped it in her mouth. "She's crazy about you. We just had a discussion about it less than five minutes ago."

Valerie felt a flicker of hope return. She got up and went to the kitchen window and saw Jackie sitting on the edge of the pool again, dangling her feet in the water.

"What is she so afraid of?" Valerie asked. "I'm never sure what to do."

"Be honest and tell her how you feel," Carla said from the table. "And tell her more than once. Tell her until she believes you. That's what she needs right now. Some positive reinforcement."

Be honest, Valerie thought with a sigh. *That's a hurdle I need to work on.* She opened the back door to stifling hot air and dropped a towel next to her at the edge of the pool. Valerie sat down and eased her feet into the cool water.

"Food's getting cold," Valerie said. She watched Jackie lean back on her arms, letting her dark brown hair fall past her shoulders. Her tan T-shirt was loose but couldn't hide the soft shape of her ample breasts.

"You never answered my question," Jackie said after a moment. She sniffed and then dabbed her eyes on the sleeve of her shirt. "What do you expect to get out of this?"

Valerie moved her feet slowly through the water, which didn't seem as cool to her any more. "Are you inquiring about my intentions toward you?" Valerie asked. "Or wondering where I think we'll be three months from now? A year from now? Ten years from now? Clarify the question a little."

Jackie didn't say anything, and Valerie was beginning to feel even more uneasy. She hadn't realized before how fragile Jackie could be. In her professional life she was so strong and confident, but the woman beside her now could at times be a complete mystery.

"How old is your mother?" Jackie asked.

"Forty-six," Valerie said, and felt a spark of anger at the slight groan she heard come from Jackie. "Don't make our ages an issue. This is—"

"I'm four years younger than your mother."

Valerie took a deep breath but didn't quite know what else to say. She wasn't about to apologize for being young and saw no point in trying to explain why she found older women so desirable.

"How many lovers have you had?" Jackie asked.

"Several."

"More than ten?"

"No." Valerie laughed and scooped water up in her hand. "What is this?"

"Were they your age?"

"Some were."

"Your longest relationship," Jackie said. "How long were you together?"

Valerie leaned back on her arms and felt the hot concrete against her palms. "Is this the conversation we tried to have the other night and never got around to?"

Jackie's lack of response was all the answer Valerie needed. "Then let me propose the same question to you," she said. "Tell me what *you* expect to get out of this." There was still no response, and Valerie began tasting the fear that slowly rose up in her throat. *Is it possible for me to lose someone solely because I love her?* she wondered. *What the hell is fair about that?*

Valerie wanted no more of this right now. If Jackie refused to talk to her, then they'd have to wait and have this scene another time. She got up and dried her legs and feet on the towel. She could feel the tears so close that she no longer trusted her voice.

"You'll eventually leave me for someone younger," Jackie said. "That's what I expect from this."

"Oh?" Valerie said as she tossed the damp towel over a lawn chair. "I think I'm the one with a bigger reason to worry about that than you are. One of the things I'll always remember about today is how I told you I loved you and all I got in return was the third degree on my old dating habits. I'm in this for the long haul, Ms. Knovac. When will you start to realize that?"

She refrained from slamming the back and the front door on her way out. This was too much to soak up in an afternoon.

Chapter Eight

Benny agreed to let Valerie drive on the way to Austin Sunday morning. If he was too nervous to eat breakfast, she knew he wouldn't be able to keep his mind on the road for very long. The stretch of interstate between San Antonio and Austin was famous for its speed traps, and neither Benny nor Valerie was in the mood to deal with authority any sooner than they had to.

They rode with the top down, oblivious to the damage to previously perfect hair. A good thirty seconds with a comb would have them presentable again. They were both dressed up for the occasion; Benny was in his light blue suit and Gucci loafers. *At least he remembered to wear socks this time*, Valerie thought. Magda had voiced her dislike for that particular fad more than once already.

Benny always looked good no matter what he wore. With some people, clothes helped shape an image or brought a particular style or persona to the surface, but with Benny the opposite was true. Anything draped on his body seemed to have class—from burlap jams to the bulky Santa suit he donned at Christmas for the Children's Hospital fund-raiser. He gave fashion a chance to maximize its potential simply by wearing something.

Designers and agents alike, a few of them ex-lovers, still called Benny on occasion, hoping to lure him back in the business, but Benny's modeling days were over years ago. That brief stint during college had upset his parents enough to get his attention. Valerie found their influence over him one of Benny's greatest weaknesses, but she had finally stopped badgering him about it. Until he was ready to get on with his life and no longer needed his parents' approval, he was stuffed forever in that crowded closet.

"How are things going with Jackie?" he asked a while later.

Valerie shrugged. *Good question.* She hadn't got much sleep the night before and was glad to have something to do today besides mope around her apartment and stare at the phone.

"Have you told her anything yet?" he asked.

"I'm laying the groundwork first."

"How much of a problem will I be?"

"Monumental," she said honestly. Valerie watched the highway and slipped easily in and out of traffic. *How do you tell your new lesbian lover that you're married to a man?* she wondered. The marriage was a farce, an elaborate scheme to ensure that Benny received his inheritance, but explaining such to someone as emotionally unpredictable as Jackie

Knovac was something Valerie hadn't been looking forward to.

Being married to Benny, a gay man already in a long-term homosexual relationship, on the surface shouldn't pose any real problem, but Valerie knew what turmoil this bit of news would cause. She firmly believed that had she told Jackie any of this in the beginning, they wouldn't be where they were now. *And where exactly am I?* she wondered. *Jackie's not ready for me to love her yet, and she thinks I'm too young. Why should she accept Colin and Benny into her life any more than she's willing to accept me?*

Valerie glanced over at Benny again and remembered wanting to help him with this marriage charade from the very beginning. There'd been no question about which female he wanted to marry if he had to marry one. There was no one safer or better for him than Valerie Dennison. She had been his only choice. The three of them—Valerie, Benny, and Colin—shared a penthouse, one whole floor of a fashionable apartment building and a stroke of designing genius on Colin's part. The penthouse had a huge common living area that they jokingly referred to as the bridal suite. This was where Valerie and Benny entertained and pretended to be the happy couple when Benny's parents came over or when they hosted something for the office. Colin was usually out for the evening during these masquerades or stayed busy in Valerie's portion of the living space. When Benny and Valerie weren't having to put on a show for the Tacketts, the bridal suite was seldom used by anyone.

Until Jackie Knovac came along, the make-believe marriage had been an amusing if not uneventful way of life. Valerie's parents were aware of the arrangement and had approved from the beginning. Their liberal nature frowned on the Tacketts' attempt to "normalize" their son by withholding what was rightfully his. Anita and Keith Dennison, Valerie's parents, had a few dreams of their own come true over this "marriage" as well. Keith Dennison got to be in his daughter's wedding—an event he had been assured on more than one occasion would never take place—and Anita Dennison had gained two sons in the process. Benny and Colin had standing invitations at all functions held in the Dennison home, as well as both of the Dennisons' vacation getaways in Aspen and Cape Cod. Everyone seemed to be happy with the arrangements.

On his thirtieth birthday, if Benjamin E. Tackett III was still married, he would receive his twenty million dollars. Valerie had been promised a generous sum, but she already had money of her own in trust with no strings attached. Benny, Valerie, and Colin had five years to go before they could dispense with their beepers. All in all, things seemed to be going pretty well.

"When do you plan to tell her?" Benny asked.

Valerie slowed the Miata down as they reached the city limits of Austin. "This week. I need to get back in her good graces first."

"Maybe the four of us should have dinner or something," he said. "Seeing Colin and me together might soften the blow a bit."

"Since when did you become such an optimist?"

He laughed. "She seems important to you. I'd like to see you happy."

"Yeah. Me, too."

Like a wavering alcoholic within reach of a drink, Valerie forced herself to stay away from the telephone for a while longer. Sunday evening she and Benny had driven back from Austin late, and Valerie hadn't got an answer when she called Jackie's house. To add further to her frustration, Jackie's answering machine never kicked in.

The next morning Valerie plucked up matching earrings from the clutter on her dresser and dropped them in the pocket of her dark blue skirt. She would finish getting accessorized in the car on the way to work. *How can I feel so wired on so little sleep?* she wondered.

Once at the office, Valerie closed the door beside her desk and postponed getting her first cup of coffee. She got comfortable in her big leather chair and reached for the phone. *Why am I so nervous?*

"Jackie Knovac," said the crisp, clear voice on the first ring.

"Good morning," Valerie managed to say. "Forgive me for calling you at work." She heard a pause and then a deep sigh.

"Good morning," Jackie said. Valerie detected a tinge of warmth in her voice and mentally crossed her fingers. "Right now I'm just grateful you're still calling me at all." Jackie laughed and took a dramatic deep breath. "I had a lousy weekend. How was yours?"

Valerie finally began to relax a little. "I've had better."

"Carla and I spent yesterday together discussing my shitty attitude. She says I'm being grossly unfair to you."

"In what way?" *Bless you, Carla!*

"For starters," Jackie said, "demanding an itinerary from you for the rest of our lives. And these little childish, stub-

94

born fits of insecurity I've been throwing. Carla doesn't understand how I can be so disciplined and successful on a professional level but so totally fucked up when it comes to my personal life." Jackie laughed again. "I think that's a direct quote. She drops these questions on me like I know the answers or something."

Through the phone Valerie could hear a knock on Jackie's door and Jackie's hasty, "Just a minute," intended for Valerie. Valerie didn't recognize the other voice. A few seconds later Jackie was back on the line again apologizing.

"It's okay," Valerie said. "The office isn't the ideal place for having this type of conversation."

"I know. Let's have dinner tonight. Someplace quiet where we can talk."

Before Valerie could say anything, Jackie added, "I was miserable when you left on Saturday. I think you gave me a scare."

"My leaving?"

"Your everything." Jackie lowered her voice. "The things you said. The things I *didn't* say. Then you were gone and I didn't hear from you yesterday. And by the way," she said pointedly, her voice rising a bit. "I still don't have an address or a phone number for you. What's the deal here?"

Valerie gave her every number she could think of—home, office, and beeper. "Stay with me at my place tonight," Valerie said. "We'll have dinner first. Someplace safe and neutral where we can talk for a while."

"I'd like that," Jackie whispered.

"Someplace where we can't get distracted by all that humping and thumping we seem to do."

Chapter Nine

All the way to the restaurant that evening Valerie was a bundle of nerves. She knew she had to tell Jackie about Benny, but she wasn't quite sure how to do it or even when the right time would be. But there was no excuse for putting it off any longer.

They arrived at the restaurant at the same time, and Valerie made no secret about how good she thought Jackie looked. Jackie was dressed casually in tan crushed-denim pants and a cream-colored sweater that emphasized her firm breasts. As Valerie met her on the sidewalk, she noticed that Jackie was checking her out as well.

"Has it only been two days since I've seen you?" Jackie asked as they fell into step. "It seems longer."

They got a table right away and scanned their menus. Valerie felt momentarily intoxicated by Jackie's perfume. *I can't sit through dinner squirming like this. Get a grip, girl.*

"How was your trip?" Jackie asked.

"Pleasingly uneventful. How's Carla?"

Jackie rolled her eyes, making them both laugh.

"Tell me more about this shitty attitude of yours," Valerie said. "Were there any conclusions drawn about this observation?"

"We'll get to that later. Let's talk about you first."

Valerie felt a brief moment of panic before she reminded herself that this was one of the reasons they were here.

"I'd like to know more about your parents," Jackie said. "What did they say when you told them about us?"

"They want to see me happy, and I assured them that with you I could be."

"Hmm."

Valerie sat up a little straighter in her chair. "There were some concerns about discretion and such, but only because of all the news about gay-bashing weirdos. They read a lot and worry about things like that."

"Being discreet is never a bad idea," Jackie said quietly. "A moment's indiscretion can ruin your life. Meeting Phyllis taught me that." She had a faraway look in her eyes before she smiled and tilted her head a little. Valerie felt that familiar tumble in her stomach all over again. "What does your father do?" Jackie asked. "Your parents sound like such interesting people."

"They work together in advertising. Have you ever heard of the Dentac Agency?"

"Of course. We've used them as consultants several—"
Jackie stopped in midsentence and glanced over at her, blinking several times. "You're not one of *the* Dennisons, are you?
Avery Dennison is your father?"

"He's my grandfather. He retired several years ago."

"Then Keith Dennison is your father," Jackie said. Her face was flushed, and Valerie noted that her eyes had widened a bit. "Keith Dennison ran for mayor in the eighties."

"Unsuccessfully," Valerie said. "And he hates being reminded of it."

"And the Tacketts," Jackie continued. "One of the oldest families in the state. The Dennisons and the Tacketts are business partners."

Christ, here she is ratting off all this stuff while I've been wondering how to bring the subject up! Valerie cleared her throat and unconsciously played with her silverware.

"I've known the Tacketts all my life," Valerie said. "Benny Tackett and I grew up together." She tried to read Jackie's expression to gauge how much of this she was ready for. "As teenagers we were inseparable. We eventually confided in each other about our sexual preferences."

"Benny Tackett is gay?"

Valerie nodded. "He had it pretty rough as a kid. Sports and girls were never his thing. He would rather spend a Saturday night doing my hair than anything else." She ran the tip of her finger down the side of her water glass. "One night he called me after a terrible fight with his grandfather and his mother. They had asked him right out if he was gay."
She lowered her voice and closed her eyes for a moment. "He was ready to kill himself that night. I woke my parents, and my father and I went over to the Tacketts' house. We got

98

into Benny's room without anyone else knowing and then took him back to our place. My mother was waiting when we got home. The four of us stayed up all night drinking hot chocolate and talking." She smiled and shook her head. "My mother was wonderful that night. She kept our mugs full and held Benny when he cried. My father kept apologizing over and over again, as if he were somehow responsible for the way some people treat their kids. I'll always believe we saved Benny's life that night."

Valerie offered another shy smile. "My parents really are remarkable people. They made suggestions about things Benny and I could do to make his life at home more tolerable. We agreed to start dating each other—going to movies, football games, skating, bowling—always secretly checking out the real action while we were together. Opportunities for Benny were much more prevalent than they were for me, though. There just didn't seem to be as many seventeen-year-old lesbians back then."

"Benny's married now, isn't he?" Jackie asked in a quiet, subdued voice. She was looking right at her.

"Yes," Valerie answered.

"And he's married to you, isn't he?"

Valerie's hand began to tremble as she reached for her water glass. She stopped and put her hands together in front of her.

"Carla told me yesterday," Jackie said. "She didn't know who he was or anything. All she really knew was that your husband was gay and needed to be married for some reason."

"D.J. must've told her," Valerie said. She didn't recognize her own voice and cleared her throat before meeting Jackie's eyes. "Benny has to stay married another five years before he

99

gets his inheritance. That's a stipulation of his grandfather's will."

"Does Benny have a lover?"

"Yes. They've been together seven years. The three of us went to Jamaica for the honeymoon." Valerie tossed a spray of curls away from her face. "You seem to be taking this pretty well."

"I've had time to think about it."

There was silence for a while, and Valerie couldn't believe how easy that had been. No tears. No scene. Nothing thrown or broken.

"I understand all too well how beneficial such arrangements can be," Jackie said. "I know a lesbian who married a gay sailor solely for commissary privileges and a free pap smear once a year."

Their food arrived, and Valerie was grateful for the momentary distraction. She poked her broiled chicken breast with her fork and managed to choke down a green bean. They both seemed comfortable with the silence.

A few minutes later, after pretending to be engrossed with her flounder, Jackie set her fork down and said, "I have two questions to ask you. Feel free not to answer either one since none of this is really any of my business."

"You can ask me anything," Valerie whispered.

"The new sports car and the Harley and the endless supply of impossible-to-get concert tickets. You're getting a monthly allowance, aren't you?"

"Yes." Valerie could feel the heat along her ears and knew her face was glowing.

"Benny's money?"

"My money. I've got a trust fund of my own."

Tears began to well up in Jackie's eyes just as Jackie looked over at Valerie. She brushed them away quickly with the back of her hand and tried to say something else, but her voice broke. Jackie put her hand up and silently asked for a little more time to compose herself. She dabbed at the tears with her napkin and looked over at her with liquid brown eyes full of gloom.

"You pretended to quit your job for me," she said slowly, hesitantly, "a job you never needed in the first place."

"What are you talking about?" Valerie said in exasperation. "Of course I needed that job. I loved that job!"

"Please don't. I'm not stupid, okay?"

"I got to see you every day," Valerie continued. "I had responsibilities and friends there. By resigning, I was risking losing you completely." She was suddenly furious that her actions had been so easily misunderstood. What the hell was happening here? "People with money need jobs too, Jackie. I can't sit on my ass all month waiting for my trust-fund check to come in. I like working. I need to work, goddamn it. I like nice things, and nice things cost money."

"Why aren't you working at the Dentac Agency?"

"And spend forty hours a week with my parents and Benny? No thanks." She stabbed another green bean with her fork. "Even though my father hates the thought of me working somewhere else, he respects my attempts at independence."

"I guess it's easy to be independent when you've got that tidy little sum guaranteed in the bank every month, isn't it?"

Valerie set her fork down with the green bean still attached to it. "What has you pissed off the most right now? My money or the job?"

"You lied to me," Jackie said through clenched teeth. She closed her eyes before new tears had a chance to roll down her cheeks.

"I don't believe this," Valerie said with a frustrated sigh. She felt tears of her own threatening. "Are we talking about the job again?"

Jackie snatched up her napkin and put it back in her lap. Valerie was still having trouble dealing with the fact that Jackie already knew about Benny.

"I needed a job, Jackie," she said in a calm, reasonable voice.

"You didn't need it like an ordinary person would need it! To most people a job means not having to eat Beenee Weenees every day. Having enough money for rent and a car payment, instead of having to choose which one gets paid this month."

"I refuse to apologize for having money," Valerie said, "and I resent your assumption that working for you didn't mean anything to me." She paused in an attempt to calm down a little. "I wanted that job," she said quietly. "I remember my first morning there. I got to work early and sat in my car sipping a cup of McDonald's coffee. I kept checking my watch so I wouldn't be late. I saw you drive up and park in one of the VIP slots. You played with your hair in the mirror and put on some lipstick." Valerie smiled at the memory. "You had on that dark blue suit of yours . . . and the skirt with the slit up the side. Jesus. I watched you drop something when you got out of the car and then you reached down to pick it up."

They looked at each other in a moment of total awareness, and the magic between them was back again. Jackie moved her plate out of the way and laced her fingers together in front of her.

"When did I know I loved you?" Valerie asked. "The ride back from the Melissa Etheridge concert." She took a bead of sweat from her water glass and pushed it along with the end of her finger. "And when did I know that I wanted you?" Valerie whispered. "That first morning in the parking lot." She let her finger slowly move down the outside of the glass, leaving a clear, sensual trail along the way.

"I knew what I might be losing when I resigned," Valerie said, "but the benefits promised to outweigh the risk. If you hadn't agreed to see me, then I'm not sure what I would've done next." Valerie met her eyes and shrugged. "But you're right. Beenee Weenees weren't in my immediate future."

Jackie slowly drummed her fingers on the starched table-cloth. "You remembered what I was wearing that day," she said with a touch of amazement. The fingers stopped drumming, and her eyes searched Valerie's as if hoping to find answers there. "I guess the question I've always wanted to ask you is, Why? I truly don't understand that. Why me? What is it about me that makes you go to all this trouble?"

"Trouble?" Valerie said. "I don't think of any of this as trouble, even though you've certainly done your best to discourage me," she noted with a laugh.

"And what keeps you coming back?"

"The possibilities," Valerie said. "I see endless possibilities for us."

"Tell me what you see."

Valerie picked up her fork and shook the green bean off. "I see you taking a chance and learning to trust someone again, and I see us someday living together." She set the fork down and looked steadily into Jackie's eyes. "I see you eventually falling in love with me. You'll fight it and deny it for a while, but you won't be able to stop yourself."

Jackie smiled and then chuckled. "Your confidence is refreshing."

Valerie was very aware that Jackie still wasn't giving her much encouragement or any reason to believe that she cared for her at all.

"You still haven't answered my question," Jackie said. She pulled her plate back and attempted to renew interest in the flounder. "Why me? You and Benny apparently have to be discreet. Why get involved with someone who's had the word *dyke* sprayed on her house?"

"You still try to protect your privacy," Valerie said. "I'm attracted to you for a number of reasons. The physical goes without saying, of course. Why someone hasn't snatched you up already is a mystery to me."

"It's my shitty attitude," Jackie said matter-of-factly. She set her fork down again and moved her plate away. "You actually remember what I was wearing that day."

They looked at each other for a long, thrilling moment, and Valerie felt her stomach do its usual fluttering somer-sault.

"It's those trivial little nonsense things you do sometimes," Jackie said. "Like knowing how I fix my coffee. Or saving my favorite doughnut for me. Those are the things that could make me fall in love with you." She folded her napkin and signaled the waiter for the check. "Not the way you press me up against the door when you kiss me good-bye," she said in a low, even voice, "or the way you run your hands over the front of my body when you come up behind me. Whose place is closer? Mine or yours?"

"Mine."

Jackie took out a crisp fifty-dollar bill and tucked it under the check.

"Is the top up or down on the Miata?" Jackie asked as she collected her purse.

"Down," Valerie said. She pushed her chair back away from the table. Apparently they were leaving.

"Then we'll go in my car," Jackie said.

Chapter Ten

As they crossed the parking lot, Valerie could feel the excitement and sexual energy practically humming in the air. She wasn't quite sure how things had progressed to this point so rapidly, but she hoped they would stay that way for a while.

"You left that guy a twenty-dollar tip," Valerie said as she opened the car door.

"There wasn't time to wait for change," Jackie said. She tossed her purse in the backseat of her car. "I'm afraid I have no shame at the moment. All I can think about is having your hands on me."

Once they were in Jackie's car, Valerie leaned over to kiss her. The parking lot had security lights attached to the outside of the restaurant behind them, but the lights fortunately weren't doing a very good job of revealing or securing anything. Jackie's mouth was possessive and her tongue teasingly demanding. She placed Valerie's hand on her breast and then moaned at the pressure of a thumb against her hardened nipple.

They blindly fumbled with their seats for a better position. The sound of heavy breathing and the rustling of clothes was just as stimulating as lips and hands on warm flesh.

"Kiss me," Jackie whispered as she leaned her head back. "Please kiss me."

Valerie had the zipper down on Jackie's pants and worked her hand inside. She found Jackie's mouth again and gently probed with her tongue. Jackie grabbed her head with both hands and kissed her hard as her hips began to move. Jackie was so hot and responsive that Valerie was sure she herself would come from just listening to her.

"Oh, yes . . ." Jackie gasped as she pulled her mouth away. She buried her face in the side of Valerie's neck and then came with a long, shuddering orgasm. Valerie held her and gladly kept her fingers in place for several minutes. If anyone had been lucky enough to hear them, there wouldn't have been a dry pair of underwear in the entire parking lot.

Valerie switched on a light in her apartment and tossed her keys on the coffee table. "Would you like something to drink?"

"No, thanks," Jackie said as she looked around the big living room. They had readjusted their clothing a second time in the parking garage at Valerie's place. Surprisingly, they both looked very presentable, considering what they'd been doing for the past forty-five minutes.

Valerie showed her around the apartment and explained how and where it connected to Benny and Colin's living space. Jackie had told her on the way over that she wanted to meet them tonight. Valerie reached for the phone; she had seen Benny's BMW and Colin's Toyota in the garage when they came in.

"Are you busy right now?" Valerie asked when Benny answered the phone. "Jackie's here and wants to meet you." Jackie came over and took her hand, causing Valerie's stomach to do another little tumble. "The bridal suite in five minutes."

Valerie hung up and took Jackie's other hand as well. They didn't have time for anything more than creative necking.

"I've never groped a married woman before," Jackie whispered before she tugged on Valerie's earlobe with her teeth.

"You've done much more than grope one, darling. Come on. Let's freshen up a bit." Valerie led the way to her bathroom. "If Colin were to get a whiff of my fingers right now I'd never hear the end of it."

Valerie couldn't have asked for a more amiable meeting between her two best friends and her lover. Colin took over and became the hostess they were all hoping for. He led Jackie on a tour of his and Benny's part of the penthouse as well as the community areas that the three of them shared. Benny and Valerie tagged along behind them, adding bits of remodeling trivia as they went.

"We both have access to the bridal suite," Benny said, "but notice how you can't really see either of the doors from the inside." There was another kitchen off to the left and down a short hallway in the back. "We've got three kitchens and three full baths. Valerie was generous enough to take the smaller apartment."

"I have everything I need," she said. Valerie watched as Benny and Jackie went to make a pot of decaf. Colin smiled and wiggled his eyebrows as she came over and sat down beside him.

"Well," he said. "How are we doing?"

"You're fine." Valerie hugged him fiercely. "I can't believe things are going so well."

"I thought you said she was a lot older than you. I was expecting Bea Arthur, and you bring us Barbara Hershey." Colin ran his finger along the top of a lamp shade, checking for dust. "She seems to be taking this thing with you and Benny pretty well."

"Yeah," Valerie said. *Almost too well.*

Jackie and Benny came back a few minutes later, with Benny laughing heartily. He wheeled in a cart with coffee, cups, cream, and an assortment of cookies.

"Jackie wants to see the wedding pictures," Benny said delightedly. "Where are they, Colin? And the honeymoon. We've got fabulous pictures of Jamaica."

An hour and a half later they were still thumbing through albums. The wedding and the honeymoon had been adequately documented and abundantly discussed. After the last picture was commented on, Jackie glanced at her watch and shrieked.

"Goodness! I had no idea it was so late."

"If you like, we can bore you with videos next time," Benny said. "Someone else did the wedding, but Colin took all the Jamaica footage."

"Videos?" Jackie said. "Hmm. I'd love to see them sometime."

Valerie stood up and took Jackie's hand. She leaned over and kissed Benny and Colin on the cheek. "You two run along. We'll clean up here."

"No way, honey," Colin said, already up and loading the coffee cart. "It was nice meeting you, Jackie. Don't be a stranger."

"Let's have dinner next week," Benny said as he helped Colin clean off the table.

"We'd like that," Jackie said. She squeezed Valerie's hand and then brought it up to her lips for a kiss.

"When can I meet your parents?" Jackie asked as they got ready for bed. She pulled her sweater off and hung it in Valerie's closet.

"Whenever you're ready," Valerie said. She smiled and lay back on the bed without bothering to undress. "They're probably still up. We could go over there now if you like."

"I need to eventually get some sleep tonight." Jackie slowly took her pants off and draped them neatly over a chair.

Valerie felt her heart rate quicken at the sight of Jackie's nude body. She cleared her throat and reached for the buttons on her own shirt. "I can make sure they're both home tomorrow evening at a reasonable time. Would that be soon enough?"

Jackie pulled her up off the bed and helped her out of her clothes. "Yes," she whispered. "Tomorrow's fine." She took Valerie's shirt and tossed it on the dresser. "I hope you're not sleepy yet."

Valerie called her mother as soon as she got to work the next morning and made arrangements for dinner at the Dennisons' that evening. Thoughts of the night before made a renewed warmth slowly spread through Valerie's body as she sat behind her desk reminiscing. Jackie had dropped her off at the restaurant early that morning to pick up her car, and their brief kiss before going their separate ways was still fresh in her mind.

She called Jackie to tell her about their dinner plans later, but Jackie was on her way to a meeting and couldn't talk right then. They made hasty arrangements for Valerie to pick her up at seven. A while later Benny called Valerie to see if she was free for lunch.

"You wouldn't believe how excited your mother is," he said as he pulled her chair out away from the table. "I was in her office for an hour this morning answering questions about you and Jackie." He opened his menu and shook his head. "She even put Colin on the speakerphone at one point because I wasn't quite as helpful as she thought I should be."

Valerie chuckled and closed her menu. "She didn't sound any different when I talked to her earlier."

"This is big, Valerie," he said seriously. "Trust me. Your mother thinks this is big. She's even making your father get a haircut today."

As soon as the waiter left with their orders, Benny reached for Valerie's hand. "Six Dentac employees just came in," he said from the side of his mouth. "Pretend you're madly in love with me."

Valerie pulled into Jackie's driveway and parked right behind Carla's new black Probe. D.J., Carla, and Jackie were there with the doors open and the trunk up.

"Do you believe anyone would buy a black car in south Texas?" Jackie said as Valerie joined them in the yard. Jackie had her hands on her hips and looked absolutely ravishing. "You'll be able to cook a pot roast in this thing come July, Carla baby."

"Maybe so, but doesn't it look great now?"

"Speaking of looking great," Valerie said, giving Jackie a lingering once-over. She wore a new burgundy dress with a semiconservative V at the neck, and her hair was tied loosely in the back with a bow made from the same material.

"I'm ready," Jackie said. "Can we put the top up on the Miata? I spent twenty minutes on this hair." Once they were out of the driveway, Jackie squeezed Valerie's hand. "I'm so nervous. Do I really look okay? I thought I could do this with no problem."

"You look great. Relax."

"What did Benny and Colin say about me today? I know you talked to them."

"Oh, yeah?" Valerie said with a laugh. "Benny and I had lunch, and I talked to Colin early this afternoon. Colin likes your sense of humor, but that doesn't really surprise me. You've both got a warped side that shows itself occasionally."

"Warped?"

The car behind them ran a red light, causing tires to screech and horns to honk. Valerie looked in her rearview mirror as a green Escort sped up and then slowed down again.

"Where do your parents live?" Jackie asked.

"The Dominion."

Jackie leaned back against the headrest and turned to look at her as panic flickered across her face. "Tell me you're kidding."

Valerie shook her head. "Sorry. That's where they live."

"Holy shit." She reached for Valerie's hand again. "Our next big discussion will have to be about money. I've been feeling a bit overwhelmed lately, I'm afraid."

Traffic out Interstate 10 was steady, and Valerie glanced up in the rearview mirror several times to still find the green Escort behind them, but they lost it when they reached the gate at the Dominion.

The guard checked Valerie's identification and let them in. She decided to take Jackie's mind off all the huge million-dollar homes by running a hand up the inside of Jackie's thigh, but it didn't seem to be working. Valerie gave in and pointed out where David Robinson and George Strait lived instead.

"Come in, come in," Anita Dennison said once they arrived. "Keith," she called down the hallway, "they're here."

Valerie let her mother take over from there; Benny and Colin had done a thorough job of briefing her. Valerie could tell by the easiness of Jackie's laugh and the way she responded to her parents' questions that things were beginning to go well.

Anita went to check on dinner a while later, and Jackie commented on how much Valerie looked like her mother.

"Yes," Keith agreed readily. "Our Valerie was very lucky in that respect." His deep laughter always made Valerie smile. She could see her father in the role of mayor or even senator some day. His graying hair and dashing good looks were almost prerequisites for any politician, and Valerie hoped he would someday change his mind about running for office again.

"I understand you've already met Benny and Colin," he said.

Jackie nodded. "Last night. They were delightful."

"Colin was over here earlier helping your mother with some sort of asparagus thing he'd told her about. Benny had another golf lesson this afternoon." Keith laughed. "Colin says our Benny even insisted on a block of instruction on how to drive the golf cart."

Dinner was wonderful and relaxing. Valerie saw no further signs of Jackie's nervousness. Dishes were left for later at Anita's insistence, and coffee and dessert were served in the living room. Anita invited them for dinner again on Saturday, when Benny and Colin would be able to make it as well.

Several hours later when they got ready to leave, Jackie let Valerie take her hand as they walked to the door. Valerie hugged her parents and thanked them for a very special evening. She felt a lump in her throat as both of the Dennisons hugged Jackie too.

"So how did it go?" Valerie asked anxiously before they were even out of the driveway.

"I should be asking you that," Jackie said. "They seemed to like me. And they're everything you said they'd be."

"Of course they like you. I'll call my mom in the morning and get a full report." Valerie laughed. "Or I can call her tonight. Would that be better?"

Jackie reached over and touched Valerie's hair and the back of her neck. "Where are we staying tonight? My place or yours?" Valerie could hear the sultry heat in her voice.

"It doesn't matter," Valerie said. "I brought a change of clothes, so I guess your place would be easier." The fingers continued caressing her hair and skin, making her want more, making her need more. By the time they arrived at Jackie's house, Valerie's nipples were hard and her thighs ached. She got her garment bag out of the back and turned around in time to see a green blur speed past the house.

Chapter Eleven

Several days later Valerie got a call from Jackie at work saying something had come up and she couldn't see her that evening.

"Is everything okay?" Valerie asked. "You sound a little stressed."

"I don't know yet. I'll call you later."

Valerie had dinner with Benny and Colin but declined their invitation for a movie afterward. She didn't want to miss Jackie's call. She puttered around her apartment and even cleaned out her refrigerator. At ten-thirty that night the phone finally rang.

"Hi," Valerie said. "Are you coming over?"

"We've got a little problem," Jackie said. "Someone's attempting to blackmail me with a set of pictures of us. She wants twenty thousand dollars or she's going to show them to your husband."

"What?" Valerie bellowed. "What are you talking about?" She sat up so quickly that she dumped her book on the floor. "Is that where you've been this evening? Meeting some weirdo?"

"She called me at work today," Jackie said. "I had to meet her. I didn't have any choice." She sighed heavily. "I made Carla and D.J. go with me though. They kept watch a few booths behind us at a coffee shop." Valerie heard Jackie's voice break as she said, "I'm so sorry about this."

"Benny won't care about any pictures!"

"And once Phyllis realizes that, where the hell do you think she'll go next?" Jackie asked. "How much would Benny pay to keep these pictures out of his mother's hands?"

"Oh, no," Valerie whispered as she collapsed back on the bed. "Phyllis? Your ex? Wacko, psycho Phyllis has pictures of us?" Their interlude in the restaurant parking lot the other night popped into her head. They'd been careless. An army of goose bumps scampered over her body at the thought of someone watching them make love. Valerie concentrated steadily for a moment on not throwing up.

"The pictures are of us by the pool in my backyard," Jackie said, as if reading her mind. "We're kissing. That's all. She was perched on the roof next door watching us."

"You're not paying this bitch any money," Valerie said.

"Let me worry about that. In the meantime, I don't think we should see each other for a while."

"What good will that do?"

"The less she knows about you and Benny, the better off we'll all be." Jackie sniffed and lowered her raggedy voice.

117

"Luckily, we're dealing with a real bozo here. If she had done her homework, we'd all be up shit creek."

"So what happens now? Handing over your money won't stop someone like this. She'll bleed you dry."

"She'll settle for less," Jackie said with confidence.

"And then go away for a while until it runs out. She'll be back for more. Don't you dare give her any money, Jackie. Call her bluff. Let her take the pictures to Benny and—"

"Are you crazy?" Jackie snapped. "And have your friends know what type of lunatic I've been involved with? Phyllis isn't something I'm very proud of, okay? I want her out of our lives and on her way somewhere else as soon as possible."

"She'll be back for more money later, and you know it."

"I'll deal with that when it happens," Jackie said. "I need to see how far she's willing to go with this."

Valerie's frustration was giving her a headache. "When can I see you again?"

"I don't know yet," Jackie said, her voice barely a whisper. "I'm so sorry, Valerie." She sighed again, and Valerie could hear faint nose blowing in the background. "I need to go. I've got a checkbook to balance and taller fences to order."

"I love you," Valerie said.

"I love you, too. I'll call you tomorrow."

Valerie held the phone a long time after Jackie hung up. *She loves me*, Valerie thought. *She finally said it.*

"What's up?" Colin asked as Valerie answered her door. He and Benny had just got in from the movie when she called him. Colin had changed into gray jogging shorts and the Betty Boop *YOU GO, GIRL* T-shirt she had got him for his birthday. The minute he stepped into the apartment, Valerie started to cry. "Hey," he said, suddenly alarmed. "It can't be that bad."

Valerie explained what was happening with Jackie. She ran her hand through her hair and then leaned her head back with a dejected sigh. "I guess I just need to vent. There's not much else I can do." She plopped down on the sofa beside him. "I wanted to talk to D.J., but I don't know how to get in touch with her without going over to Jackie's house."

Colin took her hand and gave it a comforting squeeze. "It's time, you know. Way past time, actually."

"Time for what?" Valerie asked.

"Time for Benny to come out to his family. He's leaving himself wide open for things like this."

"He won't do it," Valerie said. "And I can't ask him to. Coming out is a very personal thing, Colin. That's something he has to do on his own."

"You don't think he'd do it for you?"

Valerie got up and began pacing in front of the sofa. She'd never considered this option, and didn't even like thinking about it.

"I don't want him doing it for me. If he does anything, he needs to do it for himself."

"Well, we know what the chances of that are," Colin said dryly.

Valerie held a hand out for him and pulled Colin up off the sofa. "Thanks for coming over." She laughed and hugged him. "I don't feel any better, but thanks for coming over anyway."

"You realize, of course, that I have to go right down the hall and tell him everything we've just discussed."

119

Valerie gave a reluctant nod. She'd been aware of that when she called him. "Can you leave out the part where Benny has to tell the world he's gay?" she asked. "He'll never get to sleep with a suggestion like that hanging over him."

"You're right," Colin said as he opened the door. "I'll just stick to the part about his wife being a lesbian."

Valerie spent an hour on the phone Thursday night convincing Jackie to accept the dinner invitation to her parents' house on Saturday, but the only way Jackie would agree to go was if she arrived alone and then left by herself afterward. Valerie was more than willing to let her have things her way. At least they'd be able to see each other again. Valerie gave her a few more detailed directions and promised to get Jackie's name on the access roster at the front gate.

Valerie, Colin, and Benny rode over together in Benny's BMW. Once they arrived at the Dennisons', they could smell something marvelous cooking in the kitchen. All three oohed and aahed like a *Wheel of Fortune* audience. Colin headed toward the kitchen to help Anita with whatever was left to do, while Valerie hugged her father and explained that Jackie would be along later. Benny, Keith, and Valerie settled in the living room and had a few good laughs over Benny's recent golfing exploits.

"Clubbing balls all day sounds like a good idea to me," Valerie said. She chuckled when Benny and her father both crossed their legs at the same time. A few minutes later the doorbell rang and Valerie was up and on her way to answer it quickly.

"Hi," Jackie said. "Great directions. I wasn't really paying attention the last time I was here."

Valerie took the bottle of wine from her and closed the door. "Jesus, you look good," she said, but kept her promise not to touch her. That was another stipulation Jackie had insisted on before accepting the invitation.

"No kissing or fondling in your parents' house," Jackie had said. "Just seeing you again will be hard enough. Don't make it worse by reminding me about what I'm missing."

Valerie had agreed to all of Jackie's conditions at the time, but now that she was there looking incredibly relaxed and alluring in light-brown pants and caramel-colored silk blouse and jacket, Valerie was definitely having second thoughts. Jackie read her mind, smiled knowingly, and whispered, "Don't even think about it."

Dinner was excellent and the laughter nonstop. There were stories about Benny and Valerie. Colin and Valerie. Benny at the office and on the golf course. Stories about Valerie showing Colin how to check the oil in his car. Benny teaching Valerie how to walk in heels when they were kids and several stories Valerie hadn't heard in years. She glanced over at Jackie, saw the light back in her eyes, and wanted to keep it there forever.

"Valerie and Benny were so cute their senior year when they took those ballroom dancing lessons with us," Anita said. "I remember coming home from work one afternoon and finding the furniture moved and them dancing. Benny was singing 'Someday My Prince Will Come' at the top of his lungs."

"Still does the same thing every Wednesday night in the bridal suite," Colin said. "Benny's a great dipper."

"And as everyone can see," Benny said, motioning to his lover, "my prince has come."

"He's more like a princess, I'd say," Valerie offered.

They finished dessert and carried their coffee cups into the living room. The telephone rang a while later, and Keith Dennison answered it in the foyer. Valerie noticed his frown when he returned.

"That was Magda," he said to Benny. "She saw your car in the driveway. They're coming over for a few minutes."

Valerie watched Benny pale instantly. Just hearing his mother's name could do it to him. Valerie caught Jackie's questioning look and said, "You're in for a treat. You're about to meet my mother-in-law." She got up and stood beside Benny near the fireplace. Valerie reached down and tugged on his pant leg to see if he was wearing socks. Benny visibly cringed at the sight of his own bare ankle.

A few minutes later the doorbell rang, and in a stage whisper Colin said, "Magda and Junior are here. Everybody straighten up."

Valerie looked over at Benny and saw the fear in his eyes, but she knew how to ease it. She smiled and took his hand.

"We'll try for two, I think," she said. The tension around his mouth began to slowly disappear as he listened to her. He squeezed her hand in a silent thank you and recited his lines perfectly.

"Two?" he said. "We can stop after one if it's a boy."

"Children shouldn't grow up alone, Benny," Valerie whispered. "There's no one to split the money with."

"Mother," Benny said as Magda and Ben swept into the room. "You didn't tell me you'd be in town."

"I'm going back in the morning," Magda said. She was dressed in what Colin referred to as one of her shark suits. It was a gray skirt and jacket and looked very good on her. Valerie gave Magda and Ben, her father-in-law, each a hug.

"And you are?" Valerie heard Magda ask. She looked over just in time to see Jackie shaking Magda's hand.

"Jackie Knovac. Colin's friend."

"I see," Magda said. The bright red lipstick she always wore gave her that formidable *Maedchen in Uniform* look that Magda seemed to strive for. She glanced from Jackie back to Colin several times, and then dismissed them both like two insects she'd just discovered in fresh paint.

Magda and Ben stayed for a drink and chatted about business. Magda put her arm around Benny's waist as he walked his parents to the door. As soon as their car was safely out of the driveway, a burst of laughter rumbled through the Dennisons' house.

"Colin's friend?" Keith said as he shook a finger at Jackie. "Did anyone see Magda's face when she said that?"

"Excellent timing," Anita said, and then laughed heartily all over again. "Magda will be thinking about this for days. Colin's friend. Good job, Jackie. Good job!"

Chapter Twelve

"Colin thinks my mother knows everything," Benny said at lunch on Monday. Even though the restaurant was cool, Valerie could see the sweat popping out on his forehead. "Do you think she does?"

"Magda's no dummy," Valerie said, knowing that it wasn't what he wanted to hear. "You'll never make her happy, Benny. And it has nothing to do with you. If you went out and really got married, had a dozen kids, and made piles of money, she'd still find something wrong with you." Valerie lowered her voice. "You're trying to live up to her expectations, and that's an impossible task. No matter how good you are, you'll never be good enough for Magda Tackett."

Benny looked at her and blinked a few times as if trying to focus better on what she was saying. "You mean I may as well be gay since I'm a failure in her eyes anyway?"

"I'm saying you could find a cure for cancer and she'd browbeat you for not wearing socks. She thrives on the negative. You'll never make your mother happy, so why are you busting your butt every day trying to do it?"

"I don't know," he said, honestly confused. He shrugged and pulled a roll apart. "Because it's easy, I guess. At least it's easier than telling her I'm gay."

"Maybe someday you'll get tired of all this."

"I'm already tired of it."

"But not tired enough to do something," Valerie said. "You and Colin could have your own apartment. Take vacations without me tagging along. Hell, you could throw away your damn socks if you wanted to."

"Would you go with me if I ever decide to tell her?" he asked.

"Name the time and place. I'll even bring pom-poms."

Valerie had tried for two days to reach Jackie on the phone. At work she was either at a meeting or on her way to one, and at home her answering machine was either too full to hold any more messages or was on the outs again. By Wednesday Valerie was anxious and worried. She had to be with Benny early that afternoon, but she had already decided to see Jackie later whether Jackie liked it or not. If things went well with Benny and Magda today, this would be the end of the mandatory beeper era for everyone.

Colin had been working on Benny all along to come out to his parents and tell them everything, and to everyone's surprise, Benny suddenly seemed to be listening. Benny

talked it over thoroughly with the Dennisons and had support in every corner.

"They can't fire you," Keith Dennison said. "They can
disown you maybe, but they can't fire you."

"Because we'd hire you back," Anita informed him easily.

"I think your father will be okay with this," Keith said,
"and so will Magda eventually." He gave Benny a manly pat
on the back. "It's your decision, son. Whatever you choose to
do, we're behind you a hundred percent."

At the last minute Benny decided that he needed all three
Dennisons—Valerie, Keith, and Anita—with him when he
went to his parents' house. Colin volunteered to remain at
Keith and Anita's, like an expectant father in a waiting room.
Colin's presence always seemed to irritate Magda, and Benny
was stressed enough already. There was no need to add to
that any more than necessary.

"I think you should go with us," Valerie said, giving Colin
a hug. "He'll need you close by when it's over."

"You really think so?"

"Yes. I really think so. Trust me on this."

"Okay," Colin said, "but I'm staying in the car until it's all
over."

The five of them piled into Benny's BMW with Colin
driving and Benny twitching in the front seat beside him.
Keith, Valerie, and Anita were in the back offering words of
encouragement during the six-block trip to the Tacketts'
house. Colin took Benny's hand and held it firmly, giving him
silent encouragement as he drove.

"She hasn't bought a gun or anything recently, has she?"
Benny asked no one in particular. Conversation came to an

abrupt stop, eyebrows shot up, and questioning looks passed back and forth among them.

Anita finally chuckled and reached over to squeeze Benny's shoulder.

Valerie was so proud of him as he got out. She could tell he was nervous—they were all nervous—but at least it was happening. He was really going to do it this time.

The three Dennisons climbed out of the backseat and waited patiently as Colin finished his little pep talk from behind the steering wheel.

"Wait a minute, you guys," Benny said when the four of them finally reached the porch. Benny sat down on the top step and untied his new sneakers. He pulled his socks off and stuck them in his back pocket. "Okay. I'm ready."

Anita rang the doorbell, and Ben answered. He had a newspaper tucked under his arm and a surprised smile on his handsome face. He called upstairs to Magda to let her know they had company. Valerie kept an eye on Benny, looking for the usual signs of panic. She knew him so well, and loved him more at that moment than she ever thought possible. She tried to memorize his face and the uncertainty in his eyes. She wanted to be able to describe everything when she talked to Colin later. He deserved to be here, and being able to give Colin an accurate detail of what happened from here on was one of Valerie's main responsibilities at the moment.

"What a nice surprise," Magda said. She seemed genuinely pleased to see them. "What's the occasion? Would anyone like—"

"I have something to tell you, Mother," Benny said. His voice was deep and steady. He stood near the bay window

127

and made a point of looking right at her. "The Dennisons were kind enough to come with me for this."

Magda sat down on the sofa, as if her legs were incapable of holding her up any longer.

"Please," Ben said, motioning toward the love seat and another sofa across from where his wife was sitting. "Everyone, please sit down."

Valerie took her place beside Benny, who had chosen to remain standing. They all waited expectantly for him to continue.

"I'm gay, Mother, and I'm tired of pretending otherwise." He cleared his throat, and the only visible sign that he was the least bit nervous came from the twitching at the corner of his left eye.

Magda's gasp pierced the eerie silence, and Ben slumped in his chair and studied his son carefully for a moment.

"Why are you telling me this?" Magda asked. Her voice was cold, an unusually calm, frightening sound.

"I'm tired of living a lie."

"Why this all of a sudden?" Magda asked.

Benny cleared his throat again. "I've known since I was thirteen."

"Thirteen?"

"Are you involved with Colin?" Ben asked.

Valerie and her parents looked at Ben quickly. No one had expected him to say anything. In everyone's mind, this was a showdown between Benny and his mother. Valerie wondered how she could've forgot that Ben would be a part of it as well.

"Colin's my lover. We've been together for seven years."

Magda huffed up a little and then sat bolt upright on the sofa. "You were involved with this Colin character when you married Valerie?"

Benny nodded, and Magda's gaze left her son and settled on her daughter-in-law.

"Did you know about this?" Magda seethed. "What kind of woman are you? How could you—"

"Magda!" Anita said. "I'd be very careful if I were you."

"Has this marriage been consummated?" Magda demanded.

Benny and Valerie looked at one another and didn't quite know what to say.

"That's none of your business, Magda," Anita said.

"The stipulations of your grandfather's will are very specific, young man."

"The will states that I have to marry," Benny said. "I've done that."

"You have no marriage if it's never been consummated," Magda shot back.

"How can you prove it hasn't been?" Valerie asked. "You can't order me to the royal stirrups for a hymen check."

Keith and Anita snickered, but Valerie was furious. She eyed Magda with an unflinching, steady glare and let the years of outrage and intimidation slowly come back to her. Who did this woman think she was? Valerie and Benny had played the game longer than anyone in their right mind should have. The beepers, the mandatory lunches and dinner parties. Colin falling asleep on Valerie's couch on Christmas Eve because the Tacketts were being entertained in the bridal suite. The missed parties and birthday celebrations. Colin always on the outside looking in. None of it was fair.

"Are you getting an annulment once you reach thirty?" Magda asked. "Is that what you've come to tell us?"

"An annulment?" Valerie said. She looked over at Benny, who seemed to be as confused as she was.

"Then a divorce," Ben clarified. "Will the two of you be divorcing?"

"No," Benny said. "Not at all."

"What?" Magda bellowed. She was glaring at Valerie again. "You're encouraging this, aren't you? Why? What is it? If I didn't know better, I'd think you were after his money!" She huffed up again and clenched her jaw in anger.

"Magda," Anita warned. "I won't have you talking to my daughter that way."

"And you can't talk to my wife that way either," Benny said.

"Your wife," Magda hissed. "What kind of wife lets her husband sleep with men?"

"A wife who truly loves him," Valerie said quietly. "I'd do anything for Benny. Anything. He deserves to be happy, with or without your blessing." Valerie reached for Benny's hand, her eyes never leaving Magda's. "I hope to someday be the mother of your grandchildren, Magda. Imagine that." She felt that peaceful, easy calm wash over her as Benny squeezed her hand in return.

"As you can see," Keith noted after a moment, "they're very happy together."

"And why are you two here?" Magda asked as she pointed an accusing finger at Keith and Anita. "Damage control?"

"Your son felt like he needed friends around him for this," Anita said. "People who love him for who he really is." She studied Magda's stern expression before adding, "And you should be ashamed of yourself for it."

"Save your liberal hogwash for someone else, Anita. I should've known you'd take his side." Magda sat back and struck a dignified pose. She had a pensive expression on her face as she met Anita's gaze. "You have a beautiful daughter. Tell me why you're letting her waste her life this way. Encouraging her to stay with a man who can never be a real husband to her."

"Valerie makes her own decisions. That's something you'll have to ask her."

"It can't be the money," Magda said. "Valerie's due to inherit more than Benny will."

"You seem to be taking this much better than we expected," Anita said.

"I suppose Ben and I've known for years." She glanced across the room at Valerie and Benny still holding hands as they talked to Keith and Ben. "He was always such a sensitive child. Maybe it was a mistake not to put him in therapy."

"You know," Anita said, "I believe I read somewhere that with male homosexuals, it's generally attributed to a domineering mother."

Magda's jaw unclenched long enough to drop several inches. Anita excused herself and joined the others by the window.

"How's she doing?" Valerie asked her mother.

"I feel the need to make a suggestion," Anita said. "This is the perfect time to let them both know that you're a lesbian. Right now Magda thinks your life is totally meaningless without a fully functioning husband, and she's attempting to slip you into the gold digger category."

131

"Oh, hell," Valerie grumbled. She tugged on Benny's arm and whispered something to him. He nodded and offered her an encouraging smile.

Valerie sat down in the chair across from Magda, who was still fuming on the sofa. Magda's expression remained stern and unyielding, but Valerie had never been afraid of her.

"I have two things to say, and then I've got a favor to ask you," Valerie said. She waited a moment for some type of acknowledgment from Magda, but none came.

"Benny and I are both gay. We always have been and always will be. If you're wondering if we only got married for the money, then the answer is yes."

"You're a lesbian?" Magda said. "Oh, dear God!" She closed her eyes and rubbed her palm down over her face. "Then you're not sleeping with either of them?"

"Either of whom?"

"Benny or Colin."

Valerie's sudden laughter stopped conversation all over the room. "Of course not. What have you been thinking?"

"The three of you together . . . somehow. I don't know."

"That's pretty disgusting, Magda. We're gay, not perverts."

Magda's scowl was back.

"Then what was all of that nonsense about being the mother of my grandchildren?"

"We're approaching the twenty-first century, Magda. Having sex is no longer a prerequisite for parenthood."

"Oh," Magda said, curling up her nose a bit. "I see."

"The second thing," Valerie said, now that she had Magda's full attention. "I wonder if you realize how lucky you are to still have Benny. Gay men are dying every day,

Magda. If he hadn't met Colin and fallen in love, our Benny might not be with us now. Just think about that for a minute. Virtually thousands of parents out there would give anything to have their sons back. Alive and well. Happy and healthy. You're very lucky in many ways. Benny loves you."

Valerie looked closely at the tears welling up in Magda's eyes. *Yes*, she thought. *Maybe there's hope after all.*

"And the favor I need to ask you," Valerie said, trudging gaily forward.

Magda's expression was pained, but the scowl had finally disappeared. "Yes?"

"Colin's waiting out in the car. I'd like for you to go with me to invite him in."

Magda brushed one single tear away with her thumb and then nodded. After that, the rest was easy.

Chapter Thirteen

Valerie had the top down on the Miata as she zoomed along Loop 410. She tried Jackie's number again, but there was no answer. She didn't like any of this, and why had she even agreed to stay away from her in the first place? The closer she got to Jackie's house, the more agitated Valerie became. Seeing Carla's new car parked in the driveway behind Jackie's made her breathe a little more normally. A green Escort was parked in the street out front, and a new FOR SALE sign was prominently displayed on Jackie's lawn.

She rang the doorbell and then pounded vigorously on the door. Valerie imagined herself looking something like Fred Flintstone getting locked out of his house. Jackie yanked the door open and then leaned against it tiredly when she saw her.

"What are you doing here?"

"Pretend I'm the cavalry," Valerie said. "She's here, isn't she?" Valerie could see Jackie's answering machine blinking furiously on a table in the hallway. "Have you given her any money yet?"

"We're still negotiating." In a whisper Jackie said, "I've got her down to three thousand, but I'm hoping she'll take fifteen hundred and just go away." She was still holding the door open. "You can't stay. Go back home. I'll call you later."

"Not a chance, Ms. Knovac." Valerie went in and closed the door for her. Their bare arms touched moments before Valerie reached up and caressed the side of Jackie's face with the back of her hand. "We're not giving that crazy bitch one red cent. Let me handle this. We all know you don't bullshit well." She turned and started for the living room but found it empty. Apparently negotiations for blackmail payoffs were conducted in the kitchen.

Jackie followed after her at a steady clip, calling out Valerie's name in urgent exasperation. Valerie found Carla and D.J. on one side of the table—D.J. with arms crossed but seemingly ready for anything, while Carla glared at the red-head seated next to her.

"Well, look who's here," Phyllis said. Her smile and tan were perfect, not to mention her trim, athletic body. Phyllis wore a short, black sweatshirt with the sleeves torn out. The shirt hit her just below her jutting breasts and exposed a nice amount of flat, tanned stomach. Phyllis's cutoffs had uneven fringe surrounding muscular thighs, and Valerie found herself thoroughly disappointed at how attractive she was.

"I hope you brought some money," Phyllis said, fixing Valerie with a smile. She then flashed a wicked grin over in

Jackie's direction. "These pictures don't do your girlfriend justice, Jackie old girl. Tell me. Does she fuck as good as she looks?"

D.J. jumped up and lunged across the table, but Carla grabbed a belt loop and pulled her back.

"Everybody just sit down and chill," Jackie ordered over the ruckus. "Everybody but you," she said, pointing at Valerie. "You're leaving."

"Not yet I'm not. I need a piece of paper and a pen," Valerie said as she ignored Jackie's instructions and sat down. She eyed D.J. across the table and repeated the words *paper* and *pen*. From there she proceeded to introduce herself to Phyllis. "I'm Valerie Dennison, and I understand you have some pictures of me. Can I see them?"

Phyllis smirked and tossed her a thin Photo Mat packet. Valerie took her time with each picture, lingering over one in particular of Jackie leaning toward her with lips parted and eyes closed. "This one's good," she said. Valerie met Phyllis's dark expression with calculated boldness. "Did Jackie's neighbors give you permission to use their roof for these? If not, then expect to be brought up on trespassing charges. We'll be pursuing that later in addition to a stalking complaint and the extortion charge. That should get the police's attention." She inspected another picture of Jackie touching Valerie's wet hair, as if moving a lock away from her eyes. Valerie buried her anger at having such a personal, intimate moment reduced to this, but now wasn't the time to dwell on sentiment.

"Your shutter speed's off," Valerie said. "These are all a little too dark. First time with a zoom lens?" She picked up the pen D.J. had got for her and began writing something.

Carla, D.J., and Phyllis all craned their necks to get a better look at the paper Valerie was writing on.

"This is my husband's address and phone number in case you don't have it already," Valerie said. "He had plans with his lover and couldn't make this little meeting." She continued to scribble and caught Carla's wide-eyed surprise from her peripheral vision. "And this is my parents' address and phone number, and also here's some info on my in-laws." To D.J., Valerie smiled sweetly and said, "Benny came out to his parents this afternoon, which makes these photos absolutely worthless. I'm so proud of him." She snapped her fingers and began scribbling again. "I almost forgot. This is where I work, and here's my boss's phone number," she said to Phyllis. "Outing people at work is a specialty of yours, isn't it? We can't have you calling the wrong office and making a fool of yourself, now can we?"

Valerie tore the paper off the tablet and slid it across the table. She stood up and pushed her chair in, meeting Jackie's tired but amused eyes as she leaned against the refrigerator with her hands deep in her pockets.

Valerie nodded toward Phyllis. "Do you still have a restraining order against her?"

"I was invited here," Phyllis said. She started pitching things in a backpack and drilled Jackie with a wild, furious look. "Can I speak to you alone for a minute?"

"Not hardly," Carla said. "We've all had enough of you."

Jackie didn't move. There was a weariness in her eyes as she continued staring at Phyllis. The tan collar of her starched cotton shirt gave some color to her otherwise pale face.

"I'm not giving you any more money," Jackie said.

"Five hundred for pictures and negatives both," Phyllis said.

Jackie shook her head.

"A hundred," Phyllis suggested. "Maybe that boss of yours would be interested in seeing these."

"You want his address and phone number?" Valerie asked innocently.

Carla snatched the backpack away from her and took the pictures, negatives, and the paper with addresses on it. "Not even gas money, you maggot." She threw the backpack at her; Phyllis caught it easily with one hand and left without another word.

Carla sniffed again after apologizing for the umpteenth time about bringing Phyllis into Jackie's life in the first place. Jackie sat down in her rocking chair near the fireplace and faced the rest of them on the sofa.

"You introduced us, Carla," Jackie said. "You didn't make me sleep with her." She slowly began rocking and then sighed after a moment. "I'm not staying here tonight, and I suggest you don't either," she said to D.J. "Phyllis is crazy enough to come back and burn the house down." Jackie's gaze left D.J. and settled on Valerie, causing a landslide of tumbling in Valerie's stomach once again.

"Is there room for two at your place for a while?" Jackie asked.

"Sure," Valerie said. "My bed is your bed."

Jackie stopped rocking and then rubbed her eyes. "Let's go out for a drink. Shouldn't we be celebrating or something?"

"Colin and Benny are dancing on the tables at a club downtown by now," Valerie said. "They were in a very festive mood when I left them earlier. They shouldn't be hard to find."

Everyone was up and receptive to the suggestion. Jackie pulled Valerie into her arms and held her for a long time. Carla and D.J. joined them in the middle of the room for a group hug, all four with their heads together and arms around each other.

"Well?" Carla said, cutting her eyes over at Jackie. "Does she or doesn't she? You never answered Phyllis's question."

Jackie raised an eyebrow. "What question?"

"You know," Carla said. "The one about whether or not Valerie fucks as good as she looks."

"Oh, that question," Jackie said over everyone's laughter. "Better actually." She smiled into Valerie's glowing pink face and whispered, "Much better."

EPILOGUE
Six Years Later

Jackie carried the tray and dodged a toy dump truck in the middle of the hall. "I wonder how this got here," she said, pointing to it with the toe of her shoe. "Are they driving themselves out of your room again?"

Benjie picked it up and tucked it under his little arm. "Me and Colin were playin'. He must've forgot it." He hurried ahead of her to get the door. Setting the truck down, he wrestled with the knob, his small hands persistent and determined. Benjie was four and nothing short of a miniature version of his father. He had Benny's hair color, dark brown eyes, and that Tackett cleft chin.

"She's awake," he said excitedly over his shoulder. He pushed the door open farther and scurried inside. "Me and

Jackie made lunch," he told his mother. "Peanut butter samitches and soup."

"My favorite." Valerie threw the covers off and let Benjie help with her slippers. "I need to sit up for a while."

"Feeling any better?" Jackie asked. She set the tray on the table and gathered three chairs around it.

"I'd kill for an aspirin," Valerie said. Her swollen, pregnant body was unsuccessfully fighting off a cold. The baby wasn't due for three more weeks, and she couldn't take any medication. Valerie ruffled her son's hair and stretched a kink out of her tired, aching back. She looked down at her billowing nightgown and groaned. "I must look awful."

"You look wonderful," Jackie said. They both recognized the emotion in her voice and smiled. "Here," Jackie said. "Sit down and eat. We made samitches."

Jackie never dreamed she could be so happy. Valerie had given meaning to her life, had given her a real home and a family. The five of them—Colin, Benny, Valerie, Jackie, and Benjie—lived in an eight-bedroom, four-bath, two-story mansion in the Dominion, just down the street from Keith and Anita. The Tacketts were several blocks away in the other direction. Magda was a frequent visitor these days and had returned to the San Antonio office to be closer to her family.

Valerie first broached the subject of having a baby after she and Jackie had been together a little over a year, and Jackie surprised them all by truly being excited about the idea. She'd never thought much about babies before, nor had she spent any time with one, but there was something very special about discussing it and planning for one. Jackie found it easy to get caught up in all the enthusiasm.

144

"I want this to be your baby, too," Valerie said one night after they'd made love. She settled into Jackie's arms and hugged her. "You'll be a part of its conception and its upbringing."

"I'm old enough to be its grandmother, you know."

"A young grandmother maybe. Gravity's been very good to you," Valerie said as she ran her hand under Jackie's firm breasts. "Is that a no then?"

Jackie kissed her forehead. "It's just an observation. I guess this is one way to ensure that we'll have someone to push me around in the wheelchair when the time comes." She kissed the top of Valerie's head when she felt a tear hit her bare shoulder. "How did I get so lucky?"

Benny and Colin were just as excited as Jackie and Valerie were about having a baby. Since Benny and Valerie were already married, there was never a question about who the donor would be.

"We can do this without sex, right?" Benny asked during the first of many planning sessions.

"There'll be sex involved," Valerie said, "but not between you and me."

"Okay. Then count me in."

"Think of us as four farmers," Colin said to his lover. "Farmer Benny has the seed. Farmer Colin will harvest the seed. Farmer Jackie plants the seed, and Farmer Valerie grows the seed."

"Farmer Valerie hates this analogy," Valerie said flatly. "I'll be growing this seed for nine months while the rest of you farmers do your five-minute thing and then sit the remainder of the winter out."

Astrological charts were consulted, and peak ovulation times were plotted over several months. Colin and Jackie did most of the research, which helped institute the change in Benny's wardrobe. Jockeys were replaced by boxer shorts, and tight jeans were thrown out for that loose, zoot-suit baggy look.

"Tight clothes lower the sperm count," Jackie said. Anything technical became Colin and Jackie's responsibility. If they didn't already have an answer, then it was their job to find one.

"Here's a whole pamphlet on mucus," Jackie said, waving the brochure in the air for all to see during another preconception meeting. "We'll be looking for a certain type of mucus during the month. It says there's fertile and nonfertile." She glanced at Valerie over the top of the pamphlet. "I'll help you with this part, darling."

The four of them decided on trying to make a November baby after Colin studied zodiac signs, so in January they perfected their plan. They knew by Valerie's temperature graph approximately when in February she would be the most fertile. Turkey basters and new beepers were purchased, and ocean mood-music was specially ordered. There were throw pillows and candles everywhere in Jackie and Valerie's bedroom to add atmosphere to the conception process. Colin and Benny would be in the room next to theirs when the time came.

On February 14, Valerie took her temperature at work and then paged the other three. Jackie left a briefing with Mr. Flanagan himself to rush home and coordinate the conception procedures. Everyone arrived within two minutes of one another to squealing tires and slamming car doors.

"I think I'm nervous," Benny said on his way up the stairs. "What if I get that performance anxiety thing?" He loosened his tie and hugged Jackie and Valerie to him like an awkward adolescent.

"All you've gotta do is relax and enjoy, hon," Colin said soothingly. "I'll do the rest."

Jackie took her lover by the hand and led her to their bedroom down the hall. She closed the door and pulled Valerie close. "You look beautiful."

Valerie nuzzled her neck and breathed the sweet lingering scent of that morning's herbal shampoo and perfume. "So do you. Come on. We've got work to do."

Jackie undressed her and then slipped her own clothes off. They had discovered during one of their first practice sessions that Valerie was less self-conscious about having her knees in the air and her vagina so clinically exposed if Jackie was nude as well. Jackie theorized that if gynecologists had to conduct exams naked, procedures probably wouldn't take nearly as long.

Jackie positioned her lover in the center of the huge bed with a mountain of pillows under and around her. The ocean sounds from the CD player were very relaxing, especially with the candlelight flickering each time the central heat came on.

A few minutes later there was a knock on the door, signaling Farmer Colin's delivery of the seed. Jackie went to get the container of sperm outside the door and tried to make the technical part of the insemination as romantic as possible, but she didn't have a lot to work with in that area.

She settled comfortably between Valerie's opened legs and was careful with the container. Jackie accomplished the transfer with only slightly trembling hands, urging the sperm to swim for it before placing her baby-producing paraphernalia in a gallon-size Ziploc bag.

She rubbed Valerie's bare thighs and legs to keep the circulation going and checked her watch every few minutes or so. Valerie's pelvis had to stay elevated for twenty minutes to give everything adequate opportunity to get where it needed to be. Afterward, the pillows were tossed on the floor, and their cool, naked bodies welcomed the soft, warm blankets. They squirmed against one another and made love slowly, touching and caressing with a definite purpose in mind. Valerie knew how Jackie wanted to be kissed and was more than willing to do so. They were tuned to each other so naturally, and the thought of Valerie's body possibly making a baby as they made love was overwhelming. Jackie cried afterward, and they held each other and then cried all over again.

"Happy Valentine's Day," Valerie whispered before falling asleep. The baby-making quartet repeated the procedure again over the next two days.

During the rest of the month they stayed busy and hoped that a baby was on the way. In March when Valerie missed her period, Jackie and Colin were off to the drugstore for a pregnancy-test kit. Two were purchased just to make sure, and a nice nutritious dinner was prepared in case a celebration was in order. Colin read the directions on the box again for the tenth time while Jackie took the kit out of its wrapper. She handed Valerie what she needed, and the three of them escorted her to the bathroom. Colin, Benny, and Jackie waited outside the door for the news.

"Positive!" came the excited muffled voice from inside the bathroom. The other three were still hugging and yelling when Valerie came out waving the little stick.

"On the first try," Benny said as he strutted around and hitched up his ridiculously loose pants.

Jackie and Colin hurried to get chairs for the parents-to-be. "Here. Sit," Jackie said. "You two must be exhausted." She put her damp palm on Valerie's forehead and then kissed her quickly on the mouth. "How do you feel?"

"I'm fine. How about you?"

"Nervous. Happy." Jackie smiled and blinked away tears. "We did it! We're gonna have a baby!"

"None of that Lamaze or natural childbirth stuff," Valerie said. "Nine months from now we go to the hospital and I wake up with a baby. Everybody got that?"

Eight months later on November 19, Benjamin E. Tackett IV was born. They called him Benjie for short, even though Colin complained about the little guy being named after a K-9 movie star. And now four years later they were doing it all over again. This close to the due date, the two technical advisers were currently in charge of preparing Benjie for the arrival of a sibling.

Jackie blew on a spoonful of NoodleOs and got it all in Benjie's mouth without spilling any. "We need to rub Mom's back later," she said. "Maybe she'd like a bubble bath, too."

"Mmm," Valerie cooed. "Yes. Mom would definitely like a bubble bath."

"Me and Jackie's makin' cookies for you later," he said.

Jackie fished more NoodleOs out of the small bowl and fed them to him.

"And tomorrow she's gonna teach me and Colin and Daddy how to change a tire. Colin had a flat on his car this mornin'."

"I bet he was mad," Valerie said. "I heard it raining earlier."

Jackie laughed. "Between Triple A and his mobile phone, the weasel never felt a drop. They came and changed it with him still behind the wheel."

Valerie smiled and rubbed her stomach. "The baby's kicking. Would you like to feel her?"

Jackie knelt down beside Valerie's chair and placed Benjie's small hands on his mother's stomach. Jackie looked up at her with love in her eyes and chuckled softly when Valerie nodded toward the tray on the table and whispered, "Great samitches."

About the Author

Peggy J. Herring lives on seven acres of mesquite in south Texas with her cockatiel, hermit crabs and two wooden cats. When she isn't writing, Peggy enjoys fishing and traveling. She is the author of *Love's Harvest, Hot Check, Those Who Wait* and from Naiad Press and *Calm Before the Storm, The Comfort of Strangers* and *Beyond All Reason* from Bella Books. In addition, Peggy has contributed short stories to several Naiad anthologies, to include, *The First Time Ever, Dancing In the Dark, Lady Be Good, The Touch of Your Hand,* and *The Very Thought of You.* Peggy is currently working on a new romance titled *White Lace and Promises* to be released by Bella Books in 2004.

Once More With Feeling and *To Have and To Hold,* originally published by Naiad Press, will also be available from Bella Books in 2004.

BACK TO BASICS: A BUTCH/FEMME EROTIC JOURNEY edited by Therese Szymanski—from Bella After Dark. 314 pp.
ISBN 1-931513-35-X $12.95

SURVIVAL OF LOVE by Frankie J. Jones. 236 pp. What will Jody do when she falls in love with her best friend's daughter?
ISBN 1-931513-55-4 $12.95

DEATH BY DEATH by Claire McNab. 167 pp. 5th Denise Cleever Thriller.   ISBN 1-931513-34-1 $12.95

CAUGHT IN THE NET by Jessica Thomas. 188 pp. A wickedly observant story of mystery, danger, and love in Provincetown.
ISBN 1-931513-54-6 $12.95

DREAMS FOUND by Lyn Denison. Australian Riley embarks on a journey to meet her birth mother . . . and gains not just a family, but the love of her life.   ISBN 1-931513-58-9 $12.95

A MOMENT'S INDISCRETION by Peggy J. Herring. 154 pp. Jackie is torn between her better judgment and the overwhelming attraction she feels for Valerie.   ISBN 1-931513-59-7 $12.95

IN EVERY PORT by Karin Kallmaker. 224 pp. Jessica's sexy, adventuresome travels.   ISBN 1-931513-36-8 $12.95

TOUCHWOOD by Karin Kallmaker. 240 pp. Loving May/December romance.   ISBN 1-931513-37-6 $12.95

WATERMARK by Karin Kallmaker. 248 pp. One burning question . . . how to lead her back to love? ISBN 1-931513-38-4 $12.95

EMBRACE IN MOTION by Karin Kallmaker. 240 pp. A whirlwind love affair.   ISBN 1-931513-39-2 $12.95

ONE DEGREE OF SEPARATION by Karin Kallmaker. 232 pp. Can an Iowa City librarian find love and passion when a California girl surfs into the close-knit dyke capital of the Midwest?
ISBN 1-931513-30-9 $12.95

CRY HAVOC A Detective Franco Mystery by Baxter Clare. 240 pp. A dead hustler with a headless rooster in his lap sends Lt. L.A. Franco headfirst against Mother Love.   ISBN 1-931513931-7 $12.95

DISTANT THUNDER by Peggy J. Herring. 294 pp. Bankrobbing drifter Cordy awakens strange new feelings in Leo in this romantic tale set in the Old West.   ISBN 1-931513-28-7 $12.95

COP OUT by Claire McNab. 216 pp. 4th Detective Inspector Carol Ashton Mystery.   ISBN 1-931513-29-5 $12.95

BLOOD LINK by Claire McNab. 159 pp. 15th Detective Inspector Carol Ashton Mystery. Is Carol unwittingly playing into a deadly plan?   ISBN 1-931513-27-9 $12.95

TALK OF THE TOWN by Saxon Bennett. 239 pp. With enough beer, barbecue and B.S., anything is possible!   ISBN 1-931513-18-X $12.95

MAYBE NEXT TIME by Karin Kallmaker. 256 pp. Sabrina Starling has it all: fame, money, women—and pain. Nothing hurts like the one that got away.   ISBN 1-931513-26-0 $12.95

WHEN GOOD GIRLS GO BAD: A Motor City Thriller by Therese Szymanski. 230 pp. Brett, Randi, and Allie join forces to stop a serial killer.   ISBN 1-931513-11-2   12.95

A DAY TOO LONG: A Helen Black Mystery by Pat Welch. 328 pp. This time Helen's fate is in her own hands.
ISBN 1-931513-22-8 $12.95

THE RED LINE OF YARMALD by Diana Rivers. 256 pp. The Hadra's only hope lies in a magical red line . . . climactic sequel to *Clouds of War.*   ISBN 1-931513-23-6 $12.95

OUTSIDE THE FLOCK by Jackie Calhoun. 224 pp. Jo embraces her new love and life.   ISBN 1-931513-13-9 $12.95

LEGACY OF LOVE by Marianne K. Martin. 224 pp. Read the whole Sage Bristo story.   ISBN 1-931513-15-5 $12.95

STREET RULES: A Detective Franco Mystery by Baxter Clare. 304 pp. Gritty, fast-paced mystery with compelling Detective L.A. Franco   ISBN 1-931513-14-7 $12.95

RECOGNITION FACTOR: 4th Denise Cleever Thriller by
Claire McNab. 176 pp. Denise Cleever tracks a notorious
terrorist to America.   ISBN 1-931513-24-4 $12.95

NORA AND LIZ by Nancy Garden. 296 pp. Lesbian romance
by the author of *Annie on My Mind*.   ISBN 1931513-20-1 $12.95

MIDAS TOUCH by Frankie J. Jones. 208 pp. Sandra had
everything but love.   ISBN 1-931513-21-X $12.95

BEYOND ALL REASON by Peggy J. Herring. 240 pp. A
romance hotter than Texas.   ISBN 1-9513-25-2 $12.95

ACCIDENTAL MURDER: 14th Detective Inspector Carol
Ashton Mystery by Claire McNab. 208 pp. Carol Ashton
tracks an elusive killer.   ISBN 1-931513-16-3 $12.95

SEEDS OF FIRE: Tunnel of Light Trilogy, Book 2 by Karin
Kallmaker writing as Laura Adams. 274 pp. Intriguing sequel to
Sleight of Hand.   ISBN 1-931513-19-8 $12.95

DRIFTING AT THE BOTTOM OF THE WORLD by
Auden Bailey. 288 pp. Beautifully written first novel set in
Antarctica.   ISBN 1-931513-17-1 $12.95

CLOUDS OF WAR by Diana Rivers. 288 pp. Women unite
to defend Zelindar!   ISBN 1-931513-12-0 $12.95

DEATHS OF JOCASTA: 2nd Micky Knight Mystery by J.M.
Redmann. 408 pp. Sexy and intriguing Lambda Literary Award-
nominated mystery.   ISBN 1-931513-10-4 $12.95

LOVE IN THE BALANCE by Marianne K. Martin. 256 pp.
The classic lesbian love story, back in print! ISBN 1-931513-08-2 $12.95

THE COMFORT OF STRANGERS by Peggy J. Herring. 272 pp.
Lela's work was her passion . . . until now.   ISBN 1-931513-09-0 $12.95

CHICKEN by Paula Martinac. 208 pp. Lynn finds that the
only thing harder than being in a lesbian relationship is ending
one.   ISBN 1-931513-07-4 $11.95

TAMARACK CREEK by Jackie Calhoun. 208 pp. An intriguing
story of love and danger.   ISBN 1-931513-06-6 $11.95

DEATH BY THE RIVERSIDE: 1st Micky Knight Mystery by
J.M. Redmann. 320 pp. Finally back in print, the book that
launched the Lambda Literary Award–winning Micky Knight
mystery series.   ISBN 1-931513-05-8 $11.95